Christmas in the Woods

Matt Philip

Published by Bright Minds Books, 2024.

CHRISTMAS IN THE WOODS

First edition. September 29, 2024.

ISBN: 979-8227231949

Written by Matt Philip.

Table of Contents

Description

Christmas in the Woods follows the unforgettable adventure of three friends—Charlie, Ella, and Ben—who decide to spend Christmas camping deep in the wilderness.

What begins as a fun holiday getaway turns into a heart-pounding journey of survival when they encounter the mysterious and imposing Bucky, a wild bear with a curious nature. As they navigate snowstorms, freezing nights, and hidden secrets in the woods, Bucky becomes an unexpected guide, leading them to safety in the most magical of ways.

This is a story of friendship, courage, and the unexpected gifts nature can offer during the most wonderful time of year.

Dedication

To the brave adventurers and dreamers, young and old, who find magic in the wilderness and wonder in the unknown. May this story remind you that friendship and courage can lead you to unexpected places, and that sometimes, the wildest adventures happen when you least expect them.

And to all those who believe in the magic of the season, this is for you.

Preface

The woods have always held a special kind of magic, a world untouched by the rush of daily life. In *Christmas in the Woods*, I wanted to explore the connection between nature's mysteries and the courage it inspires within us.

This story began with the simple idea of three friends embarking on a Christmas camping trip, but it grew into a tale of resilience, trust, and the quiet wisdom of a bear named Bucky. As the characters face the unknown, they find not only the strength to survive but also the power of friendship.

I hope this book takes you on an adventure full of wonder, danger, and the warmth of the Christmas spirit.

Chapter 1: A Christmas Idea

Snowflakes drifted lazily from the sky, coating the rooftops and streets in a blanket of white. It was the middle of December, and all around the neighborhood, Christmas decorations were lighting up the night. Charlie sat by the window of his cozy house, sipping hot chocolate as he watched the snow pile up on the windowsill. His dog, Sparky, snoozed at his feet, oblivious to the world outside.

But Charlie's mind wasn't on the snow or the decorations. He had an idea—an idea that had been growing bigger and bigger in his head over the last few days. He had always loved Christmas, but this year, he wanted to do something different, something that no one else would expect. Something that would make this Christmas the most memorable one ever.

"What if," Charlie said to himself, "we spent Christmas in the woods?"

The thought thrilled him. He could picture it: a camping trip in the wilderness, surrounded by tall pine trees covered in snow, a campfire crackling as they roasted marshmallows, and the stars twinkling above. It would be an adventure, just like the stories he loved to read. And the best part? He wouldn't be going alone. His two best friends, Ella and Ben, would be right there with him.

Excited, Charlie dashed over to his desk, grabbed his phone, and quickly texted Ella and Ben. "Guys, I've got the best idea for Christmas this year. Let's go camping in the woods! It'll be an adventure!"

It didn't take long for his friends to respond.

Ella was the first to reply. "Camping for Christmas? That sounds awesome! I'm in!"

Ben's response came a few moments later. "Are you serious? In the woods? In the middle of winter? Won't it be freezing?"

Charlie grinned at Ben's cautious reply. Ben was always the one to worry, but that's what made their trio work so well. Ella was the fearless one, Ben the thinker, and Charlie was somewhere in between—a mix of curiosity and boldness.

"It won't be that bad," Charlie texted back. "We'll have warm sleeping bags, plenty of food, and we can build a fire. Plus, it'll be an adventure we'll never forget!"

There was a long pause before Ben finally replied. "Fine. But only if we bring a ton of blankets."

Charlie cheered and quickly called both of them on a group video chat to start planning. "Alright, so here's the plan," Charlie said, his excitement barely contained. "We'll go for two nights, right before Christmas Eve. We'll pack everything we need—tents, sleeping bags, food, and Christmas decorations."

"Christmas decorations?" Ben asked, raising an eyebrow.

"Of course!" Charlie replied. "Just because we're camping doesn't mean we can't have Christmas lights and ornaments. We'll hang them on the trees around our campsite."

Ella laughed. "I love it! A Christmas adventure in the wild. We'll need to pack carefully, though. My dad has some camping gear we can borrow. I'll get us a tent and some lanterns."

"Awesome," Charlie said. "I'll bring the food and decorations. Ben, you're in charge of gadgets and anything we might need for emergencies."

"Like a heater?" Ben asked hopefully.

Charlie chuckled. "Sure, if you can find one that runs on batteries."

Over the next few days, the trio busily prepared for their Christmas camping trip. Charlie raided his house for Christmas decorations—strings of lights, colorful ornaments, and even a small battery-powered tree. Ella borrowed a sturdy tent from her dad and gathered blankets, flashlights, and cooking supplies. Ben packed every piece of camping technology he could find, including a portable phone charger, a weather radio, and, much to his delight, a small electric heater.

By the time they met up at the edge of the woods on the morning of the trip, their backpacks were stuffed with supplies. The sun was just rising, casting a golden glow over the snowy landscape, and their breath hung in the cold air like little puffs of smoke.

"We're really doing this!" Ella exclaimed, her cheeks pink from the cold.

Charlie adjusted the straps on his backpack. "Yep! Let's make this the best Christmas ever."

Ben shivered as he tightened his scarf. "I still think it's going to be freezing out here, but as long as we've got the heater, I'm in."

They set off into the woods, their boots crunching through the fresh snow. Tall pine trees surrounded them, their branches heavy with snow, and the only sound was the soft whoosh of the wind through the trees. It felt like they were stepping into a winter wonderland, a place far away from the hustle and bustle of Christmas in town.

The walk to their campsite took longer than they expected, especially with all their gear, but by the time they arrived at a small clearing near a frozen stream, they were ready to set up camp. The spot was perfect—surrounded by trees and with enough space for their tent and campfire.

"Let's get the tent up first," Charlie said, already pulling out the poles.

The three friends worked together to pitch the tent, their laughter filling the air as they stumbled through the process. By the time the tent was up, the sun had dipped lower in the sky, and the air was growing colder.

Chapter 2: The Journey Begins

The next morning, the three friends woke up early, filled with excitement. The first night had gone by without any issues, and they had slept soundly in their cozy sleeping bags, warmed by the campfire's dying embers. The sun was just beginning to rise, casting a pale light through the tall pine trees, and the snow glistened like diamonds.

"Morning, everyone!" Charlie called as he crawled out of the tent and stretched. His breath hung in the air, and his cheeks were already pink from the cold.

Ella was right behind him, bundled up in layers of sweaters and a thick jacket. "It's beautiful out here," she said, gazing at the snowy landscape. "This is exactly how I imagined a Christmas camping trip would be."

Ben, however, emerged from the tent looking less enthusiastic. His hat was pulled down over his ears, and his scarf was wrapped so tightly around his neck that only his eyes peeked out. "It's freezing," he mumbled through the layers. "How do you two look so happy?"

Charlie laughed. "Come on, Ben. It's not that bad. Besides, today's the fun part! We've got the whole forest to explore."

Ella agreed. "Let's make the most of it! We've got our map, snacks, and plenty of daylight. We could even hike up to the old lookout point."

"Lookout point?" Ben asked warily. "Isn't that kind of far?"

"It's not too far," Charlie assured him, pulling the map from his backpack. He spread it out on a flat rock and pointed to a spot about two miles away. "It's up a hill, but we'll have an amazing view of the forest. We can take a break up there, and who knows, maybe we'll see some wildlife!"

At the mention of wildlife, Ben's eyes widened. "Uh, you mean like squirrels, right? Not... bears?"

Ella grinned and nudged him. "Don't worry, Ben. The chances of us running into a bear are pretty slim. They're hibernating this time of year."

Ben sighed, clearly not entirely convinced. But he nodded anyway, trusting his friends. "Alright, let's get going then. I'll lead the way if you promise not to mention bears again."

With that settled, they packed up their day bags with snacks, water, and some extra layers of clothing. Charlie folded the map and tucked it into his coat pocket, leading the way down the trail. The forest was silent except for the occasional crunch of snow beneath their boots, and the sky was a brilliant blue above them. The trees seemed to stretch endlessly in every direction, their branches dusted with snow.

"This is incredible," Charlie said, his voice filled with awe. "I can't believe we've never done this before."

Ella nodded. "Yeah, I feel like we've discovered a whole new world. It's like something out of one of those adventure books."

Ben, walking a little behind them, was quiet. He kept glancing around nervously, as if expecting something to jump out from behind a tree. Every now and then, he'd adjust the gadgets in his backpack, making sure everything was working properly. He didn't say anything, but Charlie and Ella knew that despite his nerves, Ben was glad to be there with them.

After about an hour of walking, they reached the base of the hill that led up to the lookout point. It was steeper than they expected, but the challenge only made it more exciting.

"Race you to the top!" Charlie shouted, taking off up the hill.

Ella laughed and chased after him, her boots kicking up snow behind her. "You're on!"

Ben, shaking his head, followed more slowly, muttering, "Why do I always get dragged into these things?"

The climb was tough, but by the time they reached the top, they were breathless with excitement. From the lookout point, they could see for miles. The forest stretched out below them like a sea of white, with the tops of trees swaying gently in the wind. In the distance, the frozen stream they had camped near glittered in the sunlight.

"Wow," Ella said, her eyes wide with wonder. "This is amazing."

Charlie agreed, sitting down on a rock to catch his breath. "Totally worth it."

Ben, still out of breath from the climb, plopped down beside them. "Okay, okay, I admit it," he said, trying not to sound too impressed. "This is pretty cool."

They stayed there for a while, eating snacks and chatting, enjoying the peace and beauty of the wilderness. Charlie couldn't help but feel proud. His idea of spending Christmas in the woods was turning out to be everything he had hoped for.

As they began packing up to head back to camp, Charlie noticed something odd. There were tracks in the snow—a trail of footprints that hadn't been there when they arrived. They were large and heavy, like something had passed through the area recently.

"Hey, guys," Charlie said, pointing to the tracks. "Check this out."

Ella knelt down beside the footprints. "Whoa. What do you think made these?"

Ben, who had been brushing snow off his pants, froze when he saw the tracks. "Uh... those look big. Too big for a deer. What if it's a—"

"No way," Ella said quickly, cutting him off. "It's probably just a big animal, like a moose or something. No need to panic."

Charlie examined the tracks more closely. They led off into the trees, disappearing into the thick forest. His curiosity was piqued, but something about the size of the prints made him uneasy. Still, he didn't want to scare his friends, especially Ben.

"Let's just keep going," Charlie said, standing up and brushing off his gloves. "We've got a long walk back to camp."

Ella agreed, and after one last look at the tracks, they set off down the hill. The sun was starting to dip lower in the sky, casting long shadows over the snow, and the wind had picked up, rustling the branches of the pine trees.

As they walked, the atmosphere grew quieter. The excitement from earlier in the day began to fade, replaced by a growing sense of unease. The forest seemed darker, the silence heavier, as if they were being watched.

Chapter 3: A Chilly First Night

The walk back to their campsite took longer than expected. As the sun dipped lower and lower, the temperature dropped with it, making their breaths form small clouds in the frigid air. Charlie, Ella, and Ben quickened their pace, eager to get back before nightfall. The sense of unease they'd felt after seeing the strange footprints hadn't gone away, and the growing shadows in the forest only added to the tension.

By the time they reached the clearing where they had set up camp, the sky had turned a deep, inky blue. The first stars were just beginning to appear, and the wind had picked up, causing the trees to creak and groan.

"Okay, let's get a fire going," Charlie said, trying to sound cheerful as he dropped his backpack by the tent. "It's going to be a cold night."

"I'll grab the firewood," Ella offered, already moving toward the small pile they had gathered earlier.

Ben, who had been unusually quiet during the walk back, unzipped his backpack and pulled out the small electric heater he had packed. "I think we're going to need this tonight," he said, his voice muffled by the layers of scarves wrapped around his face.

Charlie smiled. "Good thinking, Ben. But let's get the fire going too. It'll be nice to have some light."

As Ella arranged the firewood in a neat pile, Charlie crouched down and struck a match. It took a few tries, but eventually, the fire caught, and the flames began to dance, casting a warm orange glow over the snowy campsite. They gathered around the fire, grateful for the heat, and started roasting marshmallows on sticks.

"This is more like it," Ella said, grinning as she turned her marshmallow over the flames. "Nothing beats a campfire on a cold night."

Charlie nodded in agreement, but his eyes kept flicking toward the edge of the clearing, where the trees stood tall and dark. Something about the way the wind rustled through the branches, making them sway and creak, felt different tonight. More eerie.

Ben, who had been fiddling with the heater, finally sat down beside them. "I don't know about you guys," he said, lowering his voice, "but I can't stop thinking about those tracks we saw."

Ella shrugged, clearly trying to downplay the situation. "It's probably nothing. Like I said, it's most likely just a moose or some other big animal."

Charlie wasn't so sure, but he didn't want to make Ben more nervous. "Yeah, it's probably nothing. Let's just enjoy the campfire."

For a while, they sat in silence, staring into the flames and enjoying the warmth. The crackling of the fire and the occasional gust of wind were the only sounds. But as the night wore on, the temperature continued to drop. Even with the fire and Ben's little heater, the cold seemed to seep into their bones.

"I think we should call it a night," Charlie said finally, noticing that his fingers were starting to go numb, despite his gloves. "We can bundle up in the tent and stay warm."

Ella and Ben agreed, and after making sure the fire was safely out, they retreated to the tent. It was a tight fit with all three of them inside, but they didn't mind. The closer they were, the warmer they would be.

Charlie zipped up his sleeping bag and nestled down inside it, pulling the hood over his head to block out the cold. "Night, guys," he mumbled, already feeling sleep tugging at him.

"Goodnight," Ella and Ben replied in unison.

For a while, everything was peaceful. The wind outside the tent had died down, and the soft rustling of the trees became a soothing background noise. Charlie began to drift off, his mind filled with thoughts of Christmas and the fun they would have in the morning, hiking through the woods and exploring new places.

But then, just as he was on the edge of sleep, he heard it—a low, rumbling sound, almost like a growl.

Charlie's eyes snapped open, and he held his breath, straining to listen. Had he imagined it? The wind had started to pick up again, howling through the trees. Maybe that was all it was. Just the wind.

He was about to close his eyes when he heard it again—louder this time. A definite growl, coming from somewhere outside the tent.

"Did you hear that?" Ben whispered, his voice trembling.

"Yeah," Charlie replied, trying to keep his voice steady. "I heard it."

Ella, who had been quiet, suddenly sat up in her sleeping bag. "What was that?"

None of them moved for a few moments, too scared to even breathe. Outside, the growling sound came again, closer this time. It was followed by the sound of heavy footsteps crunching through the snow, moving slowly around the tent.

Charlie's heart was racing. His mind flashed back to the footprints they had seen earlier that day. Had something been following them after all?

"What do we do?" Ben whispered, his voice barely audible.

Charlie swallowed hard. "We stay quiet," he said softly. "Maybe it'll go away."

For what felt like hours, the three friends sat huddled together in the dark, listening to the sounds outside the tent. The growling and footsteps circled the campsite, as if whatever was out there was inspecting their tent, trying to decide whether they were a threat—or a meal.

Charlie's mind raced. Could it be a bear? He had read stories about bears waking up from hibernation early if they were disturbed or hungry. The thought made his stomach twist in fear.

Just when it seemed like the tension was unbearable, the footsteps stopped. The growling faded, and the forest grew silent once more, save for the wind rustling the trees.

Charlie let out a shaky breath. "I think it's gone."

Ben peeked out of his sleeping bag, his eyes wide. "Are you sure?"

"I think so," Charlie said, though his heart was still pounding.

Ella sat back down slowly, wrapping her arms around her knees. "Whatever it was, it didn't attack us. Maybe it was just curious."

They stayed awake for a while longer, listening for any more signs of danger, but nothing else happened. Eventually, exhaustion won out, and one by one, they fell back asleep, though it was a restless sleep filled with strange dreams.

Outside the tent, the forest remained quiet, but in the distance, under the cover of night, something was still watching.

Chapter 4: Footprints in the Snow

The next morning, the forest was still and quiet, but the memories of the night before lingered heavily in the cold air. Charlie was the first to wake up, blinking groggily as the light of dawn seeped through the thin fabric of the tent. The events of the previous night came rushing back, and his heart skipped a beat. Had it all been a dream? He listened carefully, but the only sounds were the soft snores of his friends and the gentle breeze brushing the trees.

Charlie sat up, careful not to disturb Ella and Ben, who were still bundled tightly in their sleeping bags. He unzipped the tent and stepped outside into the chilly morning air. The world outside was a blanket of white, untouched except for their campsite—and something else.

His breath caught in his throat. In the snow, just beyond the edges of their tent, were large footprints. The kind he had hoped they wouldn't see again. He knelt down beside them, inspecting the tracks more closely. They were deep and wide, spaced far apart as if whatever had made them was large and lumbering.

Charlie's stomach churned as he followed the trail with his eyes. The footprints led from the edge of the forest, circled around their tent, and then disappeared back into the trees.

"Charlie? What are you looking at?"

He turned to see Ella standing in the tent's entrance, rubbing her eyes. Ben was just behind her, looking half-awake and already shivering from the cold.

Charlie pointed to the footprints. "Look."

Ella stepped forward, her eyes widening as she took in the sight. "Whoa. Those weren't there last night."

"Nope," Charlie said grimly. "Whatever was out there... it was definitely real."

Ben, who had been sleepily tugging on his boots, froze when he heard this. "Wait… those are… what I think they are, right?" He didn't even need to finish his sentence. It was obvious what he meant.

"Maybe," Ella said, crouching beside the tracks. "I'm no expert, but these look too big to be anything like a deer or moose. It looks like… like a bear."

Ben's face turned pale. "A bear? But I thought they hibernated during winter!"

"They're supposed to," Charlie replied, trying to keep his voice calm. "But sometimes they wake up early if they're disturbed or hungry. I've read about it. It's rare, though."

Ella glanced back toward the forest. "We should be careful. If it's hungry, it might come back."

Ben gulped audibly. "Great. So now we've got to worry about a bear wandering around while we're trying to sleep. Fantastic."

"We'll be fine," Charlie said, trying to reassure his friend. "We'll keep the fire going at night, and we've got plenty of supplies. Plus, we'll just stay alert."

Ben didn't look convinced, but he nodded slowly. "Alright… but I'm sleeping with my emergency whistle under my pillow from now on."

Ella chuckled. "Good idea. Let's just hope we don't need to use it."

They spent the next hour eating breakfast in uneasy silence. The usual excitement they had felt the previous day had dimmed, replaced by a growing awareness of how alone they truly were in the woods. The snow-covered trees that had once seemed beautiful and magical now felt tall and imposing, as though they were hiding secrets in their shadows.

After breakfast, the trio decided to explore the area a bit more, hoping to distract themselves from the lingering tension. They bundled up in their warmest clothes and set off down a trail that wound deeper into the forest. The fresh snow crunched beneath their boots, and every so often, a branch would snap under the weight of ice, startling them.

As they walked, Charlie kept glancing over his shoulder, his nerves still on edge from the night before. But the forest remained quiet, and after a while, they began to relax a little.

"I think we're okay," Ella said, breaking the silence. "Whatever was here last night is probably long gone."

Charlie nodded, though he wasn't entirely sure. Still, he didn't want to worry Ben any more than necessary. "Yeah, maybe it just wandered by and didn't find anything interesting."

They continued hiking until they came across a frozen stream, its surface glittering in the mid-morning sun. It was a beautiful spot, and they decided to take a break there, sitting on a fallen log by the bank.

"This is nice," Ella said, taking in the view. "It's easy to forget about all the creepy stuff when you're sitting in a place like this."

Ben, who had been uncharacteristically quiet, nodded in agreement. "Yeah. I guess the woods aren't all bad."

They sat in comfortable silence for a while, listening to the soft rustling of the trees and the occasional distant call of a bird. Charlie started to feel like things might actually turn out okay. Maybe the bear—if that's what it was—had just been passing through. Maybe they wouldn't see it again.

But as they started to gather their things and prepare to head back to camp, something caught Charlie's eye. On the far side of the frozen stream, where the snow was untouched, there was another set of tracks. Large ones.

"Guys," Charlie said, his voice tense. "Look over there."

Ella and Ben followed his gaze and saw them immediately. More footprints, just like the ones by their tent. They led away from the stream and into the dense trees beyond, disappearing into the forest.

"That's the same tracks," Ella said, her brow furrowed. "It's been following the stream."

Ben groaned, already reaching for his emergency whistle. "This just keeps getting better and better."

Charlie stood up, his mind racing. If the bear was following the stream, there was no telling how close it was to their campsite—or how often it had been circling around. The thought of it creeping through the woods at night, just feet from where they slept, sent a chill down his spine.

"We should head back," Charlie said firmly. "We need to figure out a plan in case it comes too close."

They gathered their things quickly and set off back toward the camp, their earlier calm shattered by the discovery of the tracks. The walk back felt longer this time, every rustle of the trees and crunch of snow putting them on edge. Charlie kept scanning the forest, half-expecting to see something large and dark moving between the trees.

When they finally reached their campsite, the fire they had left smoldering had gone out. Everything was exactly as they had left it—except for one thing.

There, right by the entrance to their tent, were fresh footprints in the snow.

The bear had been back while they were gone.

Chapter 5: A Mysterious Visitor

The sight of the fresh footprints near the tent sent a wave of cold fear through Charlie, Ella, and Ben. The snow around the tent was perfectly untouched, except for the large, unmistakable prints that circled it like a predator stalking its prey. Whatever had made those tracks had come back—and it had done so while they were gone.

Ben took a step back, his eyes wide. "This is getting worse by the minute. What if it comes back while we're here?"

Charlie swallowed hard, his mind racing. The bear, if that's what it was, had clearly been investigating their camp. But why? What had drawn it here? He looked around the clearing, trying to think of anything that might have attracted the creature. Then it hit him—the food.

"It's probably looking for food," Charlie said, thinking out loud. "We left our supplies out in the open. Maybe the smell brought it here."

Ella's eyes widened as she looked toward the small pile of food they had stored near the tent. "You think that's what it's after?"

Ben grabbed his emergency whistle and clutched it tightly. "Great, so now we're not just dealing with a bear, but a *hungry* bear. We should've stayed home and watched Christmas movies."

Charlie forced a smile, though his nerves were frayed. "We'll be fine, Ben. We just need to be smart about this." He pointed to the food. "First, let's move everything up into the trees. If we hang it high enough, the bear won't be able to reach it."

"That's a good idea," Ella said, already moving to gather the supplies.

The three of them worked quickly, packing up their food and tying it into secure bundles. They found a tall, sturdy tree near the edge of the campsite and, with some effort, managed to hoist the supplies up high enough to keep them out of the bear's reach.

Once the food was safely stored, they gathered around the fire pit, keeping a watchful eye on the forest. The trees stood tall and silent, casting long shadows over the snow. Every rustle of the wind through the branches made them tense, half-expecting the bear to appear at any moment.

"I hate this," Ben muttered, pulling his jacket tighter around him. "It's like we're sitting ducks out here."

"We'll be okay," Charlie said, trying to sound more confident than he felt. "Bears don't usually attack people. They're just looking for food. As long as we're careful and don't leave anything out, it'll lose interest."

Ella nodded in agreement. "Yeah, and if it does come back, we can make noise to scare it off. Bears don't like loud noises."

Ben looked down at the whistle in his hand. "You're sure about that, right?"

Ella smiled. "Positive."

The day passed slowly. They spent most of it huddled around the fire, taking turns keeping watch for any sign of movement in the woods. The lighthearted fun they had hoped for on this Christmas camping trip had been replaced with a gnawing sense of unease. It wasn't what any of them had imagined.

As the sun began to sink behind the trees, casting the sky in shades of orange and pink, Charlie stood up and stretched. "We need to rebuild the fire. It's going to get really cold again tonight."

Ella nodded. "I'll help you gather wood."

Ben, who had been unusually quiet, looked at them with wide eyes. "You're not going out there, are you? What if it comes back?"

Charlie sighed. "We don't have a choice, Ben. We need to stay warm tonight. We'll be quick."

Reluctantly, Ben nodded and stayed by the fire while Charlie and Ella ventured a little deeper into the forest, gathering fallen branches and twigs to keep the fire going. They moved swiftly, their eyes scanning the trees for any signs of movement.

"I think we'll be okay," Ella said softly as she snapped a twig over her knee. "I don't think it'll come back tonight."

Charlie wasn't so sure, but he nodded anyway. "Let's just be quick."

They gathered enough wood to last the night and hurried back to camp. Ben was still sitting by the fire, his whistle clutched tightly in his hand, his eyes darting nervously between the trees. "You were gone for a while," he said, his voice shaky. "I thought... I thought something happened."

Charlie set down the bundle of wood and smiled. "We're fine, Ben. Everything's fine."

But even as he said it, Charlie couldn't shake the feeling that they were being watched. Something about the forest seemed different—quieter, as though the animals had all gone into hiding. His gut told him that the bear wasn't far away.

They rebuilt the fire and settled down for the night, huddled close to the warmth. The small tent behind them seemed like it offered little protection, but none of them wanted to go inside yet. Not while the forest felt so ominous.

"I wonder why it came back," Ben mused after a long silence. "If it didn't find food, why would it keep coming here?"

"I don't know," Ella replied, her voice thoughtful. "Maybe it's curious about us."

Charlie didn't respond. His eyes were locked on the edge of the clearing, where the firelight met the dark shadows of the trees. And then, without warning, he saw it—a dark shape, moving slowly between the trunks. His breath caught in his throat.

"There!" he whispered urgently, pointing toward the trees. "Look!"

Ella and Ben turned sharply, following his gaze. And there, just at the edge of the clearing, a large bear stepped into view. Its thick fur was covered in patches of snow, and its eyes gleamed in the dim light of the fire.

Ben's hand shot to his whistle, but Charlie held up a hand. "Wait," he whispered. "Don't blow it yet."

The bear didn't seem aggressive. It stood at the edge of the clearing, watching them with dark, curious eyes. It wasn't the kind of wild, snarling bear they had imagined. In fact, it almost seemed hesitant, as if unsure whether it should approach.

Ella slowly stood up, her movements calm and steady. "It's okay," she said quietly, almost as if she were talking to the bear. "It's not here to hurt us."

Ben, who looked ready to bolt, glanced nervously at her. "How do you know?"

"I don't know," she admitted. "But it's not acting like it wants to attack."

For what felt like an eternity, the three friends stood frozen, watching the bear as it sniffed the air and took a cautious step forward. Then, just as suddenly as it had appeared, the bear turned and lumbered back into the trees, disappearing into the shadows.

The trio let out a collective breath of relief.

"What just happened?" Ben whispered, still clutching his whistle.

"I don't know," Charlie replied, shaking his head in disbelief. "But I think we just met our visitor."

Chapter 6: Meeting Bucky

Charlie, Ella, and Ben gathered around the fire pit, huddled in their jackets as they warmed their hands. None of them had said much since waking up, and the tension was palpable.

Finally, Ben broke the silence. "So... what was that last night? It didn't attack us, but it didn't run away either. What do we do now?"

Ella poked at the dying embers with a stick, her face thoughtful. "I don't know. I've never heard of a bear acting like that before. It almost seemed... curious."

Charlie nodded in agreement. "Yeah. It didn't seem like it wanted to hurt us. If it did, it would have come closer, right?"

Ben wasn't convinced. "Or maybe it's just waiting for the right moment."

Ella shook her head. "I don't think so. If it wanted to attack, it would've done it by now."

Charlie stood up and stretched. "I say we stay alert but try to go about our day. We can't just sit here and wait for it to come back. Let's explore a bit more, maybe head toward the stream again."

Ben looked uneasy but nodded. "As long as we don't go too far."

They packed a few supplies and set out toward the frozen stream, keeping a close eye on their surroundings. The forest, though quiet, didn't seem as threatening in the daylight. The tall trees and thick blanket of snow made it feel more like a winter wonderland than the ominous woods they had encountered the night before.

As they walked, the conversation shifted back to the bear.

"Maybe it's not dangerous," Ella suggested. "Maybe it's just lonely. It's odd for a bear to be awake in the winter, after all."

Charlie smiled, though he wasn't entirely sure if Ella was joking or not. "A lonely bear? I guess it's possible."

Ben, on the other hand, was still tense. "Lonely or not, it's still a bear. We need to be careful."

When they reached the stream, they paused to admire the view again. The frozen water stretched out before them, glittering under the pale winter sun. They sat down on a fallen log, resting for a while as they chatted about their plans for the rest of the trip.

Suddenly, there was a rustling sound from the trees behind them.

All three of them froze.

"Do you hear that?" Charlie whispered.

They turned slowly, their eyes scanning the tree line. At first, they saw nothing. But then, from behind a cluster of snow-covered bushes, the bear appeared again. It was the same one from the night before, large and lumbering, its dark fur standing out against the white snow.

Ben instinctively reached for his whistle, but Charlie grabbed his arm. "Wait."

The bear stopped at the edge of the clearing, watching them. Its gaze was steady, curious even, but it didn't move closer. It just stood there, sniffing the air as if trying to figure out what they were.

Ella stood up slowly, making sure not to startle the animal. "I don't think it's here to hurt us."

Ben stared at her, his eyes wide with disbelief. "Ella, are you crazy? It's a *bear*!"

Charlie watched the bear carefully. It was big, yes, but something about the way it moved—slowly, almost lazily—made him think that Ella might be right. There was no aggression in its stance, no sign that it was about to charge.

"I think Ella's right," Charlie said quietly. "It's not acting like a predator."

The bear took a few cautious steps forward, its nose twitching as it sniffed the air again. It didn't seem afraid of them, but it didn't seem aggressive either.

Ella took a deep breath and, to Charlie and Ben's shock, took a step toward the bear.

"Ella, what are you doing?!" Ben hissed, his hand still gripping the whistle.

Ella didn't respond. She knelt down in the snow, keeping her movements slow and deliberate, and held out her hand as if offering the bear a sign of peace. The bear paused, its eyes locking onto her. Then, to their astonishment, it took another step forward.

Charlie held his breath, unsure of what would happen next. But the bear didn't attack. It simply stood there, watching them with its dark, intelligent eyes.

For a long moment, no one moved. The bear seemed to be studying them, trying to figure out what they were doing in its forest. And then, as if satisfied, it turned and lumbered back toward the trees, disappearing into the shadows once more.

Ella let out a breath she hadn't realized she was holding. "Did... did that just happen?"

Charlie nodded, still in disbelief. "Yeah. That just happened."

Ben, who had been frozen in place the entire time, finally found his voice. "We need to name it."

Ella and Charlie both turned to stare at him. "What?" they said in unison.

Ben shrugged, still looking a little shaken. "I mean, if it's not going to eat us, it should have a name. You know, like a mascot or something."

Charlie chuckled, relieved to hear Ben's sense of humor returning. "Alright, what do you want to call it?"

Ben thought for a moment. "How about Bucky?"

"Bucky?" Ella repeated, raising an eyebrow.

Ben nodded. "Yeah. Bucky the Bear."

Charlie laughed. "Bucky it is, then."

Ella grinned. "Okay, fine. Bucky it is. But I don't think Bucky's going to be our pet bear. We still need to be careful."

They sat back down on the log, the tension of the moment slowly fading. It was strange, but after that encounter, they didn't feel quite as afraid. The bear—Bucky—hadn't attacked them. In fact, it seemed more curious than anything else. Maybe Ella was right. Maybe Bucky wasn't dangerous. Maybe he was just as confused by their presence as they were by his.

"I guess Bucky's our new camping buddy," Charlie said with a smile. "As long as he doesn't get too close."

Ben nodded, still looking a bit uneasy but less terrified than before. "I can live with that."

For the rest of the day, they stayed near the stream, talking about Bucky and what their next move should be. While they knew they still had to be cautious, the fear that had gripped them before was starting to lift. Maybe this Christmas in the woods wasn't going to be as dangerous as they thought.

Chapter 7: Trouble in the Forest

The sun had barely begun to dip below the horizon when the wind picked up, swirling the snowflakes into the air like tiny, white sparks. What had been a peaceful day was quickly transforming into something far more threatening. The trio stood around the campfire, which flickered weakly against the sharp gusts of wind, sending shadows dancing across the snow.

"I don't like this," Ben said, tugging his hat down over his ears. "The wind's getting stronger, and the sky looks like it's about to dump more snow on us."

Ella nodded, her gaze drifting toward the darkening clouds. "Yeah, this feels like a storm. We should probably hunker down for the night."

Charlie agreed. "Let's pack up everything that could get blown away. We need to secure the tent and make sure we've got enough wood to keep the fire going."

They moved quickly, the tension in the air thickening as the first few flakes of snow began to fall. Charlie and Ella worked together to secure the tent's ropes, tying them down to nearby trees to make sure the tent wouldn't collapse in the wind. Meanwhile, Ben gathered as much firewood as he could find, though the wind made it increasingly difficult to keep the fire burning strong.

By the time they finished, the snow was coming down in earnest, thick and fast. The wind howled through the trees, and the temperature seemed to drop with every passing minute.

"This is bad," Ben said, standing close to the fire and rubbing his hands together. "We should've brought an extra tent or something. If the storm gets worse, I don't know how we're going to stay warm."

Charlie glanced at the pile of wood they'd gathered. It wasn't nearly enough to last through the night, not with the fire struggling to stay lit in the wind. "We'll be fine," he said, trying to sound confident. "We've got warm clothes, sleeping bags, and the tent. We just need to ride this out."

But even as he said it, the wind gusted harder, sending a shiver down his spine. The tent flapped violently in the storm, and Charlie wasn't entirely sure it would hold through the night. The snow was already starting to pile up around them, covering the ground and making it harder to move.

Ella huddled closer to the fire, but her eyes were fixed on the trees. "Do you think Bucky's still out there?"

Ben glanced up, his face pale. "You think the bear's going to come back in this storm?"

Charlie shook his head. "No, I doubt it. Animals usually take shelter during bad weather. He's probably hunkered down somewhere, just like we should be."

But as the storm intensified, Charlie found himself wondering if that was really the case. If Bucky had already come so close to their camp once, what was stopping him from returning? And what if the storm drove him closer, searching for food or shelter?

The wind whipped snow into their faces, and Charlie realized they couldn't stay outside any longer. "We need to get into the tent," he said firmly. "This fire's not going to last much longer."

Ella and Ben didn't argue. They quickly grabbed their backpacks and crawled inside the tent, zipping it up tightly against the cold. Inside, it was warmer, but the howling wind outside made the tent feel flimsy and fragile.

Charlie pulled his sleeping bag around him and tried to get comfortable, but the constant flapping of the tent's fabric made it hard to relax. Ella sat cross-legged beside him, her face illuminated by the dim glow of the lantern they had brought inside.

"We should keep watch," she suggested. "Take turns staying awake. Just in case."

Ben looked horrified. "In case of what? The storm? Or... Bucky?"

Ella shrugged. "Both."

Charlie sighed. "I don't think Bucky's coming back tonight. But you're right—we should take shifts, just to be safe."

They decided on a rotation, with Ella taking the first shift, followed by Charlie, and then Ben. As the storm raged outside, Charlie closed his eyes and tried to sleep, though his mind was racing. The wind roared, shaking the tent and sending gusts of cold air through the seams. Snow piled up against the sides of the tent, making it feel even more isolated from the world outside.

Ella kept watch, her eyes darting between the tent flaps and the shadows outside. She could hear the wind howling and the trees creaking, but beyond that, the world was eerily silent. The storm had chased away any sounds of wildlife, leaving only the angry voice of the wind and the soft rustle of snow.

Hours passed, though it was hard to tell exactly how much time had gone by. Finally, Ella shook Charlie awake, signaling that it was his turn to keep watch. Charlie sat up, still groggy, and rubbed his eyes as Ella snuggled into her sleeping bag.

As he sat in the dim light of the lantern, Charlie's mind wandered back to Bucky. The bear hadn't acted like a typical wild animal—there had been something more in its eyes, a kind of intelligence that Charlie hadn't expected. It was as if Bucky had been trying to understand them, just as they were trying to understand him.

Charlie listened to the storm outside, the wind rattling the trees and the snow piling higher against the tent. His thoughts were interrupted by a sudden noise—a low, rumbling growl that seemed to come from just outside the tent.

He froze, his heart pounding. Had he imagined it? Or had Bucky come back after all?

He leaned closer to the tent flap, straining to listen. The growling sound came again, louder this time. It was unmistakable.

Charlie's blood turned to ice. He quickly shook Ella and Ben awake, his voice barely above a whisper. "Guys. I think Bucky's back."

Ella sat up, her eyes wide with alarm. "Are you sure?"

Before Charlie could answer, the growling came again, followed by the unmistakable sound of heavy footsteps crunching through the snow, circling the tent.

Ben scrambled for his emergency whistle, his hands trembling as he gripped it tightly. "What do we do?" he whispered.

Charlie's mind raced. The storm had grown so intense that leaving the tent wasn't an option. They were trapped, with nothing but thin fabric between them and the bear.

The footsteps outside stopped, and for a moment, there was only silence. Then, with a soft huff, the bear moved away from the tent, its footsteps fading into the distance.

The three friends sat in stunned silence, their hearts racing. Finally, Ben let out a shaky breath. "Is... is it gone?"

Charlie nodded, though he wasn't entirely sure. "I think so."

Ella looked toward the tent flap, her eyes filled with both fear and curiosity. "What is Bucky doing? Why does he keep coming back?"

Charlie didn't have an answer. But one thing was clear—their unexpected visitor wasn't finished with them yet.

Chapter 8: Navigating the Wild

The morning after the storm was eerily calm. The wind had died down, and the sky was a bright, icy blue, but the forest felt different. The snow lay thick and heavy on the ground, making every step crunch loudly in the stillness. The trees were bent under the weight of the snow, and icicles hung from the branches, glittering in the early light.

Charlie, Ella, and Ben emerged from the tent, bleary-eyed and tense from the long, restless night. The storm had passed, but the memory of Bucky circling their tent in the middle of the night still weighed heavily on their minds.

Ben looked around at the snowdrifts that had piled up overnight. "That was... intense," he said, his voice shaky. "I thought for sure the tent was going to collapse."

"It held up better than I expected," Ella said, stretching her arms and rubbing her cold hands together. "But I'm more worried about Bucky. He was so close last night."

Charlie scanned the area, looking for any signs of the bear, but all he saw were the footprints left behind in the snow. Bucky had come and gone again, just as mysteriously as before.

"I don't get it," Charlie said, frowning. "He didn't attack, but he didn't stay away either. Why does he keep coming back?"

"Maybe it's the food," Ben suggested, pointing toward the tree where they had hung their supplies. "But he didn't try to take it."

Ella shrugged. "Maybe he's just curious. We're strangers in his territory, after all."

Whatever the reason, the encounter with Bucky left them all on edge. They had come here expecting a peaceful, adventurous Christmas in the woods, but now, things felt unpredictable. The bear's presence loomed over them like a shadow, and though Bucky hadn't shown aggression, the fact that he was so close—and kept returning—made it impossible to fully relax.

"We need to move," Charlie said finally. "If Bucky keeps coming back, it might be better for us to find another campsite, at least until we figure out what's going on."

Ben's eyes widened. "You mean pack up everything and hike somewhere else? In this snow?"

Charlie nodded. "Yeah. It's not safe to stay here if Bucky keeps showing up. We'll find a better spot, maybe closer to the stream or deeper in the forest."

Ella agreed. "It's risky, but we can't just wait around for him to come back. The storm's over, so we should be able to make good progress today."

Reluctantly, Ben nodded, though he clearly wasn't thrilled with the idea. "Fine. But let's not go too far. I don't want to get lost in the middle of nowhere with that bear following us."

They packed up their gear quickly, shoving sleeping bags and supplies into their backpacks. The snow was deep, making the work harder, but they moved with a sense of urgency. The memory of Bucky's visit lingered, pushing them to leave their current camp behind as soon as possible.

Once everything was packed, they set off toward the stream, their boots sinking into the thick snow with every step. The path was slow going, the snowdrifts making it hard to navigate, but the fresh air and sunlight helped lift their spirits a little.

After about an hour of trudging through the forest, they came upon a small clearing by the frozen stream, which was covered in a layer of glittering ice. The area seemed peaceful, with tall trees surrounding it like a natural shelter.

"This looks like a good spot," Charlie said, his breath puffing in the cold air. "We can set up camp here. It's a bit more open, and we'll be closer to the stream."

Ella nodded, surveying the area. "It's perfect. We can gather water from the stream if we melt some snow, and there's plenty of wood for a fire."

They set to work, unpacking their gear and pitching the tent. The cold air nipped at their faces, but the sun overhead made the day feel brighter than the stormy, tense night they had just survived. The new campsite felt like a fresh start.

As they worked, Ben kept glancing over his shoulder, as if expecting Bucky to appear at any moment. "What if he follows us here?" he asked, his voice full of nervous energy. "What if he tracks us through the snow?"

Charlie stopped and looked at the tracks they'd left behind. It was true that their footprints would be easy to follow, especially for a bear, but so far, there was no sign of Bucky. "We'll be careful," Charlie said. "But I don't think he's after us. He's just curious."

"Curious or not, it's still a bear," Ben muttered, his shoulders hunched against the cold.

Ella gave Ben a reassuring smile. "Don't worry, Ben. We'll keep the fire going tonight, and if Bucky does show up, we'll make plenty of noise to scare him off."

After they had finished setting up camp, they sat around the fire, grateful for the warmth and the chance to rest. The stream gurgled softly beneath its icy shell, and the sound of the water gave the forest a peaceful, serene quality. For a moment, it felt like everything was back to normal.

But as the afternoon wore on, the peace began to feel fragile. Every now and then, Charlie caught himself glancing at the trees, half-expecting to see Bucky's dark shape moving through the forest. The tension from the night before hadn't completely left him, and he could tell that Ella and Ben felt the same way.

They spent the day gathering firewood and making sure their supplies were secure, but as the sun began to set, the familiar anxiety started creeping back. The forest, which had felt so open and welcoming during the day, once again took on a more sinister tone as the shadows lengthened and the temperature dropped.

As dusk settled over the forest, Charlie, Ella, and Ben huddled close to the fire, their faces illuminated by its flickering light. The world around them grew darker and quieter, and the sounds of the forest seemed to fade into the background.

"I wish we knew more about Bucky," Ella said quietly, breaking the silence. "I can't shake the feeling that he's more than just a random bear."

Charlie nodded. "Yeah, there's something different about him. I've never heard of a bear acting the way he does."

Ben, who had been staring into the fire, looked up. "Maybe we should just leave. I mean, we've had our adventure. Maybe it's time to head home."

Charlie considered this, but something inside him resisted the idea of leaving so soon. There was still something about the forest—about Bucky—that felt unfinished. "Let's stay one more night," Charlie said. "If Bucky doesn't show up again, we'll be fine. And if he does... well, maybe we can figure out what he wants."

Ben didn't look convinced, but he didn't argue. "Fine. One more night."

The night closed in around them, and as the fire crackled and popped, the trio settled into an uneasy silence. The forest outside was quiet—too quiet. Every rustle of wind through the trees made them jump, and every snap of a branch sent their hearts racing.

And then, just as they were beginning to relax, a low growl rumbled from the edge of the clearing. The three friends froze, their eyes widening in fear.

Bucky was back.

Chapter 9: The Ice River

The growl cut through the cold night air like a warning. Charlie, Ella, and Ben sat frozen around the fire, their eyes darting toward the edge of the clearing where the sound had come from. There, in the dim light of the fire, they saw the unmistakable dark shape of Bucky emerging from the shadows. His thick fur was dusted with snow, and his large, curious eyes reflected the firelight as he took a few tentative steps closer.

Ben's hand went instinctively to his emergency whistle, but Charlie held up a hand, signaling for him to wait. "Let's not scare him yet," Charlie whispered. "He didn't hurt us last time."

Ella, her breath steady but her heart racing, nodded in agreement. "Maybe he's just passing by."

Bucky stopped a few yards away from them, his massive frame looming in the darkness. For a moment, he seemed to study them, his snout twitching as he sniffed the air. The tension was thick, and though Bucky showed no signs of aggression, the sheer size of him made it impossible for them to feel at ease.

Charlie kept his eyes on the bear, his mind racing. "He's not leaving," Charlie whispered. "I think we need to move."

Ben looked horrified. "Move? As in leave the campsite? Where are we supposed to go?"

"The stream," Ella said quickly, her voice hushed but firm. "If we can make it across the ice, we'll put some distance between us and Bucky. He won't follow us onto the frozen river."

It was a bold plan, but in the back of his mind, Charlie knew it was their best option. Bucky wasn't acting aggressive, but the bear's unpredictable nature kept them on edge. If they stayed, the situation could escalate, and none of them wanted to wait and see how it played out.

"Alright," Charlie said, keeping his voice low. "We'll make our way to the stream, slowly. No sudden movements."

With their plan set, the three friends began to edge away from the fire. They moved carefully, one step at a time, trying not to startle Bucky. The bear watched them with interest but made no move to follow. His eyes tracked them as they retreated toward the tree line, their breaths puffing out in small clouds of cold air.

As they reached the edge of the clearing, Charlie turned to glance back at Bucky. The bear was still standing near the fire, sniffing at the air but showing no intention of charging. Charlie let out a silent breath of relief. Maybe, just maybe, they could get away without causing a confrontation.

But the moment they stepped into the trees, Bucky let out a low, rumbling growl. Charlie's heart skipped a beat. He looked over at Ella and Ben, their eyes wide with fear.

"He's following us," Ben whispered, his voice trembling.

"We need to hurry," Ella said, her voice tense but steady. "The stream's not far. If we can get across, we'll be safe."

They picked up their pace, moving as quickly as they could through the snow-covered forest. The trees blurred past them as they weaved through the dense undergrowth, their footsteps muffled by the thick snow. Behind them, the sound of heavy footsteps crunching through the snow told them that Bucky was still on their trail.

The stream came into view just ahead, its surface frozen solid and shimmering in the pale moonlight. Charlie's heart raced as they approached the edge. The ice looked sturdy, but the thought of crossing it while a massive bear followed close behind sent a jolt of fear through him.

"We'll go one at a time," Ella said, already stepping onto the ice. "Move quickly but carefully. If the ice cracks, we need to spread out our weight."

Charlie nodded and followed her onto the frozen surface. The ice groaned softly beneath his boots, but it held firm. They moved cautiously, testing each step as they made their way across the wide stretch of ice. The stream was much larger than it had appeared from their campsite, and the thought of falling through sent a shiver down Charlie's spine.

Ben hesitated at the edge, looking back toward the trees. "What about Bucky?" he asked, his voice barely audible. "What if he tries to follow us?"

Charlie glanced back at the dark shape of the bear, who had stopped at the edge of the stream. Bucky was standing there, watching them, but he made no move to step onto the ice. Instead, he let out a low huff and paced back and forth, as if unsure of what to do.

"I don't think he'll cross," Charlie said, relief flooding through him. "Bears don't like ice. They're too heavy—they know it's risky."

Ella was already halfway across the stream, moving steadily. "Just keep going. We'll make it to the other side, and Bucky will lose interest."

Ben, though still nervous, took a deep breath and stepped onto the ice. The surface creaked under his weight, but like the others, he moved cautiously, keeping his eyes fixed on the far bank.

As they neared the center of the frozen stream, the air felt colder, and the wind whipped across the open space, stinging their faces. Charlie kept glancing over his shoulder, half-expecting Bucky to take a sudden leap onto the ice, but the bear remained on the shore, pacing in frustration.

Just when it seemed like they were in the clear, a sharp crack echoed through the air. Charlie froze, his heart leaping into his throat.

"The ice!" Ben cried, his voice high with panic.

Charlie looked down to see a web of cracks spreading out from beneath Ben's feet. The ice was beginning to give way.

"Ben, move! Quickly!" Ella called from the far bank, her voice urgent.

Ben's face went pale as he tried to move forward, but with every step, the ice groaned louder. The cracks widened, and cold water began to seep up through the surface.

"Don't run!" Charlie shouted, trying to keep calm. "Stay low—spread your weight!"

Ben dropped to his knees, his movements shaky as he crawled forward. The ice continued to crack beneath him, but he moved slowly, inching his way across the treacherous surface. Charlie and Ella watched in tense silence, their hearts pounding in their chests.

Finally, after what felt like an eternity, Ben reached the far bank. He scrambled onto solid ground, his face flushed with relief and fear. "That... was too close," he gasped, his breath coming in ragged puffs.

Charlie and Ella quickly joined him on the far bank, their legs shaking with adrenaline. They collapsed onto the snow, their bodies aching from the cold and the tension.

For a long moment, none of them spoke. The only sound was the wind whistling through the trees and the distant rumble of the frozen stream shifting beneath the ice.

Bucky, still on the far side of the stream, watched them for a moment longer before turning and lumbering back into the woods. The bear had lost interest—at least for now.

Chapter 10: A New Shelter

After their harrowing escape across the ice, Charlie, Ella, and Ben were exhausted. The deep cold seeped into their bones, and their muscles ached from the tension of navigating the treacherous frozen stream. The forest around them, though eerily quiet, offered no sense of safety. They knew Bucky might still be out there, lurking in the shadows, and they needed to find shelter fast.

Charlie scanned their surroundings, trying to think of a plan. The frozen stream had provided them a temporary escape, but they couldn't stay exposed in the open for long. They had to find somewhere they could hide out, somewhere warmer where they could rest and recover.

"I'm freezing," Ben muttered, his teeth chattering as he pulled his scarf tighter around his neck. "We need to get out of the cold. The sun's going down again."

Ella nodded in agreement. "Yeah, and we can't risk another night without proper shelter. If we don't find something soon, we'll be in real trouble."

Charlie pointed ahead, where the trees thickened into a dense grove. "There's got to be something up ahead—maybe an old cabin or a cave. We can't stay out here all night."

With that, they trudged forward, moving deeper into the forest. The snow crunched beneath their boots, and the trees closed in around them, creating a dark, wintry maze. Every so often, Charlie glanced over his shoulder, half-expecting to see Bucky's hulking shape following them through the trees. But there was no sign of the bear.

The minutes ticked by, and the cold became even more biting. Charlie's fingers and toes felt numb, and Ben's breathing had turned into shallow gasps as the chill began to wear them all down. Just when it seemed like they couldn't go on any longer, Ella suddenly stopped in her tracks.

"Look!" she exclaimed, pointing ahead.

Through the trees, barely visible beneath a thick layer of snow, stood an old, weathered cabin. The wooden structure was nestled between two large pines, its roof sagging under the weight of the snow, but it was still standing. Smoke no longer curled from its chimney, and its windows were dark, but it looked like it could provide the shelter they so desperately needed.

Charlie's heart lifted. "That's perfect! Come on!"

They hurried toward the cabin, their boots sinking into the deep snow as they approached. Up close, the cabin looked even older, with moss-covered logs and shutters that hung crookedly from the windows. But it was still solid, and the sight of it filled them with relief.

Charlie tested the door. It creaked open with a loud groan, and a gust of cold air blew out from inside, carrying with it the scent of pine and damp wood. The interior was dimly lit by what little daylight remained, but they could see enough to know that it was empty—and safe.

"Let's get inside," Ella said, stepping through the doorway. "It's not much, but it's better than being out in the open."

They all followed her inside, grateful to be out of the wind and snow. The cabin's single room was simple but sturdy. There was an old stone fireplace on one wall, a rickety table and two chairs in the center, and a few shelves lined with dusty jars and forgotten trinkets. A small, creaky bed sat in one corner, its mattress covered in a layer of dust.

"We can make a fire in the fireplace," Charlie suggested, already searching for wood. "It'll keep us warm tonight."

Ben, who had been shivering uncontrollably, nodded eagerly. "Yes, please. I don't care what else happens, I just need to get warm."

Ella joined Charlie in gathering wood. They found a small pile of logs stacked against the back wall of the cabin, and after clearing out the old ashes from the fireplace, they managed to get a fire going. The warmth from the flames spread through the room, and for the first time in hours, they began to feel their frozen limbs thawing.

Ben sat as close to the fire as possible, holding his hands over the flames. "I thought I was going to turn into an icicle out there."

Charlie chuckled as he pulled out a few snacks from his backpack. "At least we found this place. It's actually kind of cozy."

Ella smiled as she set up their small camping stove on the table. "Yeah, and with the fire going, we can cook something warm. We'll be fine here for the night."

They sat around the fire, eating their meal and enjoying the warmth. The cabin's walls sheltered them from the wind, and the fire crackled softly, filling the space with light and heat. For a moment, it felt like they were safe. The tension that had gripped them since their encounter with Bucky seemed to fade, and they allowed themselves to relax, just a little.

But even as they rested, a question hung in the air—what was Bucky's connection to all of this? The bear had followed them so persistently, yet had never attacked. It was almost as if Bucky had been guiding them somewhere, watching them from a distance without showing hostility.

"I've been thinking," Charlie said, breaking the silence. "Bucky's been following us, but he hasn't done anything aggressive. It's almost like he's trying to get our attention."

Ben shivered, though not from the cold. "You're saying he's, what, leading us somewhere?"

Ella frowned thoughtfully. "It does seem strange. Maybe he's trying to tell us something. Animals can be smarter than we give them credit for."

Charlie stared into the fire, his mind racing. The strange behavior of the bear, the fact that they had stumbled upon this cabin just when they needed it most—something felt connected. But what?

As the fire crackled and the wind howled outside, they all settled into an uneasy silence. Ben stretched out on the small bed, while Ella and Charlie sat near the fire, warming their hands. Despite the warmth of the cabin, a deep sense of uncertainty lingered in the air.

"I guess we'll find out tomorrow," Charlie said softly, glancing toward the window. "Whatever Bucky's after, we'll be ready."

Ella nodded, though her expression remained thoughtful. "Let's just hope he doesn't show up in the middle of the night."

They stayed awake for a little while longer, listening to the wind outside and the occasional creak of the cabin's wooden beams. The night was quiet, save for the steady crackle of the fire. Soon, exhaustion took over, and one by one, they fell into a deep, dreamless sleep.

Outside, the snow continued to fall, and the forest remained still. But somewhere in the shadows, Bucky waited, his dark eyes watching from the edge of the woods.

Chapter 11: Celebrating in the Cabin

The sun had barely risen when Charlie woke to the soft glow of the fire, now just embers, crackling in the hearth. The small cabin was warm, and for a brief moment, he forgot where they were—the harsh cold, the strange presence of Bucky, all of it felt like a distant dream.

But then the weight of their situation hit him again.

Sitting up, he glanced at Ella and Ben, still sound asleep in their sleeping bags near the fire. They had made it through the night without incident, and the sense of relief that washed over Charlie was profound. He stretched, stood up, and looked out the small, grimy window. The forest was blanketed in a fresh layer of snow, and the sun was just peeking through the trees, casting long shadows across the untouched white.

As Charlie moved quietly around the cabin, trying not to wake his friends, his mind wandered to Bucky. The bear had disappeared after their escape across the frozen stream, but Charlie couldn't shake the feeling that they hadn't seen the last of him.

Ella stirred and blinked her eyes open. "Morning," she said, rubbing her eyes and sitting up. "Did anything happen overnight?"

Charlie shook his head. "No, it's been quiet. But we should get moving soon. We still don't know what Bucky's going to do next."

Ben groaned as he woke up, stretching his stiff limbs. "Can we at least have breakfast first? I'm starving."

Ella laughed. "Yeah, let's eat something. We need our energy if we're going to head back today."

The three of them sat around the low table, pulling out the last of their food supplies. As they ate, the cabin felt almost cozy, like a small holiday retreat far from the worries of the world. The fire, which they stoked again, crackled softly, and the warmth filled the room, pushing away the biting cold of the forest.

"I was thinking," Ella said between bites of an energy bar. "Why don't we decorate the cabin? I know it's not exactly home, but we brought Christmas decorations with us, didn't we? It might be nice to celebrate a little, even out here."

Ben raised an eyebrow. "You want to celebrate Christmas *here*? In the middle of nowhere, with a bear following us?"

Ella shrugged, her eyes sparkling. "Why not? It's still Christmas Eve. We might as well make the most of it."

Charlie considered the idea. It felt strange, celebrating in a place that wasn't home, but there was something about it that made sense. They had come here for an adventure, and while things hadn't gone as planned, they were still together. Why not embrace the moment?

"Yeah," Charlie said with a smile. "Let's do it. It'll make this Christmas one to remember."

Ben sighed but smiled, too. "Alright, fine. Let's celebrate. But if Bucky shows up, I'm not sharing my hot chocolate."

They all laughed, the tension easing for the first time in what felt like days. With a new sense of purpose, they unpacked the few decorations they had brought with them—a small string of battery-powered lights, a handful of colorful ornaments, and a tiny plastic Christmas tree.

They strung the lights around the wooden beams of the cabin, their soft glow adding a cheerful warmth to the room. The ornaments hung from the windowsills and door frame, and the little tree, though barely a foot tall, was placed proudly on the table next to the fire. It wasn't much, but it was enough to make the cabin feel festive.

As they finished decorating, Ella stood back and admired their work. "It's not like home, but it's kind of perfect, don't you think?"

Charlie nodded, his heart warming at the sight. "Yeah, it's definitely different, but in a good way."

Ben, who had been quietly sipping his hot chocolate, looked around at the cozy, decorated cabin. "You know," he said, "this isn't so bad. I mean, it's kind of cool spending Christmas in a cabin in the middle of the woods. I'll bet no one else in our class has ever done something like this."

Charlie laughed. "Definitely not. We'll have the best Christmas story to tell when we get home."

The fire crackled merrily, and for a little while, they allowed themselves to forget about the dangers lurking outside. They sat around the fire, telling stories and laughing, the weight of the past few days lifting from their shoulders.

As the day wore on, they even exchanged small gifts. Charlie had brought a small notebook for Ella, knowing how much she loved to sketch nature scenes. Ben, ever the gadget lover, gave them both small solar-powered flashlights he had packed as backups. Ella, in return, surprised them with tiny ornaments she had made from twigs and pinecones she had gathered during their hike.

"This is amazing," Ella said, her smile wide. "I didn't think we'd be able to celebrate Christmas out here, but it's turning out to be one of the best ones yet."

Charlie agreed. The warmth of the cabin, the laughter they shared—it was a moment he would never forget. Despite the fear and uncertainty they had faced, this simple Christmas celebration made everything feel right again.

But as the light outside began to fade and the sun dipped low in the sky, the reality of their situation began to creep back into their minds. Charlie stared out the window, his gaze drifting toward the darkening forest. Bucky hadn't returned, but the question of why the bear had followed them remained unanswered.

"We should still be careful tonight," Charlie said softly, breaking the cheerful mood. "Bucky could come back."

Ben frowned, his earlier smile fading. "Do you really think he will? I mean, we haven't seen him since we crossed the stream."

Ella, who had been hanging another ornament, paused. "Maybe he won't. But we should keep watch just in case."

They all knew it was a possibility. Bucky had followed them before, and while the bear hadn't shown any outright aggression, the uncertainty of his behavior was unnerving. They couldn't let their guard down completely, even during their makeshift celebration.

As the night wore on, the cabin grew quieter, the fire crackling softly as they huddled in their sleeping bags. The festive decorations hung around the room, glowing faintly in the firelight, but outside, the forest was dark and still.

The quiet stretched on, and soon the exhaustion of the day began to weigh on them. One by one, they drifted off to sleep, the warmth of the fire and the comfort of the cabin lulling them into a sense of peace.

But outside, in the darkness of the woods, something stirred. The soft crunch of snow underfoot echoed faintly through the trees. Bucky was still out there, watching, waiting.

Chapter 12: Another Bear Encounter

The silence of the night was suddenly broken by the sound of something heavy moving outside the cabin. Charlie stirred in his sleeping bag, his eyes snapping open in the dim glow of the fire's dying embers. At first, he thought he had imagined it, but then there it was again—the unmistakable sound of snow crunching underfoot, slow and deliberate.

He sat up carefully, trying not to disturb Ella and Ben, who were still fast asleep beside him. His heart began to race as he strained to listen. The footsteps were coming closer, circling the cabin just as they had circled their tent on that first night.

Charlie's breath caught in his throat. Bucky was back.

He reached over and gently shook Ella's shoulder. "Ella," he whispered urgently. "Wake up."

Ella stirred, blinking groggily as she pushed herself up. "What's going on?"

"Shh," Charlie whispered, pointing toward the window. "He's back. Bucky."

Ella's eyes widened, and she quickly sat up, her senses now fully alert. She listened carefully, and sure enough, the sound of the bear's slow, heavy footsteps was unmistakable. Bucky was pacing outside the cabin, just as he had done before, and the thought of him being so close sent a shiver down her spine.

"Do we wake Ben?" Ella whispered.

Charlie hesitated for a moment before nodding. "Yeah, but let's keep quiet. We don't want to scare Bucky—or Ben."

Ella reached over and nudged Ben awake. He opened his eyes and frowned, rubbing his face. "What now?" he mumbled.

"Bucky's outside," Ella said softly.

Ben sat up instantly, his face draining of color. "Are you serious?"

Charlie nodded, trying to stay calm. "He's circling the cabin, but I don't think he's trying to get in. He's just... watching us."

Ben's hand instinctively reached for his emergency whistle, clutching it tightly. "Why does he keep following us?"

Charlie shook his head. "I don't know. But I don't think he's going to hurt us. He hasn't tried to break in or attack. He's just curious."

The three friends sat huddled together in the small cabin, listening to the slow, steady crunch of Bucky's footsteps outside. The bear seemed to be pacing, moving around the cabin in wide circles as though he were inspecting it. The tension was unbearable, and every creak of the wooden walls made them jump.

"We need to do something," Ben whispered, his voice trembling. "We can't just sit here and wait for him to leave."

Ella glanced toward the window, where the faint outline of the bear could be seen through the frost-covered glass. "I have an idea," she said, her voice low but steady. "Maybe we should go outside and show him we're not afraid. If we confront him calmly, he might lose interest."

Ben stared at her as if she had just suggested jumping into a pit of alligators. "Go outside? Are you out of your mind? He's a *bear*, Ella!"

Charlie, though nervous, could see the logic in Ella's idea. "She might be right. Bucky's been watching us for days, but he hasn't done anything threatening. If we show him that we're not scared, maybe he'll leave us alone."

Ben looked horrified, but he knew they couldn't stay inside forever. "Fine," he muttered. "But I'm staying close to the door."

Ella stood up first, grabbing a flashlight from her bag. She took a deep breath and moved toward the door, her heart pounding in her chest. Charlie followed close behind, and though Ben reluctantly joined them, his grip on the whistle was so tight that his knuckles were white.

The wind outside had calmed, and the moonlight bathed the snowy forest in a silvery glow. As Ella slowly opened the cabin door, the cold air rushed in, and they stepped outside, their breaths visible in the freezing night.

Bucky was there, standing at the edge of the clearing, his massive frame silhouetted against the moonlit snow. His dark eyes gleamed as he watched them, but he didn't move. The air was tense, the silence broken only by the soft crunch of the snow beneath their boots as they stepped out of the cabin.

Ella raised the flashlight and shone it on Bucky, keeping her movements slow and steady. "We're not here to hurt you," she said softly, her voice barely above a whisper. "We just want to know what you want."

Bucky blinked, his head tilting slightly as if he were trying to understand her words. He didn't growl or move aggressively—he just stood there, watching them with a curious expression. The tension in the air was palpable, but there was something strange about the way Bucky looked at them, something almost... thoughtful.

Charlie, emboldened by Bucky's calm behavior, took a step forward. "Maybe he's been trying to lead us somewhere," Charlie suggested quietly. "What if he's trying to show us something?"

Ben, still clutching his whistle like a lifeline, shook his head. "Lead us? Are you kidding? He's a *bear*. Bears don't lead people anywhere—they just eat them."

But Ella didn't seem convinced. She took another slow step forward, holding her hand out, as if offering Bucky a gesture of peace. "I think Charlie's right," she said, her eyes locked on the bear. "He's been following us for days, but he hasn't hurt us. Maybe there's something we're missing."

Bucky huffed softly, his breath rising in a cloud of steam as he sniffed the air. Then, to their surprise, he turned and started to walk away, heading toward the trees on the far side of the clearing. He didn't run or disappear into the forest—he just walked, slow and deliberate, as if expecting them to follow.

Charlie's heart pounded in his chest. "Is he... trying to lead us somewhere?"

Ella nodded, her eyes wide with a mixture of awe and confusion. "I think so."

Ben, still looking like he might pass out from fear, glanced between his friends and the retreating bear. "You're not seriously thinking about following him, are you?"

Charlie and Ella exchanged a glance. "We've come this far," Charlie said. "I think we should see where he's leading us."

Ben groaned but reluctantly followed as Ella and Charlie moved to follow Bucky into the woods. The bear, though large and intimidating, moved with surprising grace as he led them deeper into the forest, his massive paws making barely a sound in the soft snow.

The moonlight filtered through the trees, casting long shadows across the snow-covered ground. The air was still, and the only sound was the crunch of their boots and the soft padding of Bucky's paws.

They followed Bucky for what felt like an eternity, the forest around them growing darker and more mysterious with every step. Charlie's mind raced—where was Bucky leading them? And why? The bear had been acting so strangely, as though he had a purpose, a reason for following them.

Then, just as the tension reached its peak, Bucky stopped at the edge of a small clearing. There, in the center of the clearing, stood something that made Charlie's heart skip a beat—an old stone structure, half-buried in the snow, its walls covered in frost and vines.

"What is this place?" Ella whispered, her voice full of awe.

Charlie stepped closer, his eyes wide with wonder. "I don't know... but I think this is what Bucky wanted us to find."

The bear stood at the edge of the clearing, watching them silently. He had led them here, to this mysterious structure, for reasons they couldn't yet understand.

Chapter 13: Lost and Found

The clearing where Bucky had led them was like something out of a dream. The snow-covered stone structure stood silently before them, half-hidden by the forest and time itself. It was larger than they had expected, with crumbling walls and arched doorways that seemed to beckon them closer. Thick vines clung to the stone, and snow weighed down the branches of nearby trees, casting strange shadows across the clearing.

Charlie, Ella, and Ben stood frozen at the edge of the clearing, their eyes wide with wonder and confusion. Bucky, the bear who had led them here, sat on his haunches near the tree line, watching them intently. He made no move to come closer, but there was a strange sense of purpose in his gaze, as if he had brought them here for a reason.

Charlie was the first to speak, his voice barely a whisper. "What is this place?"

Ella took a few tentative steps forward, her breath visible in the cold air. "It looks like some kind of old building. Maybe a cabin, or even a fort?"

Ben, who was still gripping his emergency whistle tightly, shook his head in disbelief. "You're telling me this bear—this *bear*—just led us to an ancient ruin in the middle of the forest?"

Charlie nodded slowly, his eyes fixed on the structure. "It sure seems like it. But why?"

Ella approached the stone building, her curiosity overtaking her caution. The stone walls were covered in moss, but beneath the overgrowth, she could see the faint outlines of carvings—symbols she didn't recognize. "Look at this," she called softly. "These symbols—they look really old."

Charlie and Ben joined her, studying the strange carvings. They were faint and weathered by time, but there was something about them that felt significant, as if this place had been important long ago.

"What do you think this place was?" Ben asked, still glancing nervously back at Bucky, who hadn't moved from his spot near the trees.

"I don't know," Ella replied. "But it's definitely not just some random ruin. Someone—or something—built this a long time ago."

Charlie's eyes drifted back to Bucky, who was watching them with quiet intensity. "Do you think this is why Bucky's been following us? To lead us here?"

Ella shrugged. "Maybe. It seems like he wanted us to find this place. But why?"

Ben, who was still unconvinced about the bear's mysterious behavior, crossed his arms. "I don't care why he brought us here. I just want to know if it's safe."

Charlie stepped closer to the entrance of the building, peering into the dark interior. The air inside was colder, and the smell of damp stone filled his nose. It was hard to see much beyond the entrance, but there was something about the place that felt inviting, despite its mysterious nature.

"I think we should go inside," Charlie said, his voice steady. "Maybe we'll find some answers."

Ben looked horrified. "Go *inside*? Are you crazy? This place could collapse at any moment!"

Ella, who had already moved to the entrance, smiled. "It looks pretty sturdy to me. Besides, we didn't come all this way just to stand outside."

Charlie grinned, and despite his nerves, he felt a rush of excitement. "Come on, Ben. What's the worst that could happen?"

Ben sighed, knowing he couldn't argue with both of them. "Fine," he muttered. "But if anything weird happens, I'm out of here."

Together, the three friends stepped through the arched doorway and into the stone structure. Inside, the air was still and quiet, and the walls seemed to hum with an ancient energy. Snow had piled up in the corners of the room, and vines crawled through cracks in the stone, but the structure itself remained intact.

As they moved deeper into the building, they noticed that the carvings on the walls grew more intricate. The symbols seemed to tell a story, though none of them could decipher it. There were figures—animals, people, and strange shapes—etched into the stone, and though they were worn with age, they radiated a sense of importance.

Ella ran her fingers gently over one of the carvings. "These symbols... they're like nothing I've ever seen. They look almost like they were left here as a message."

Charlie nodded, fascinated. "Maybe this place is connected to the forest somehow. Like a sacred site."

Ben, who had been nervously watching the entrance, glanced at the carvings but didn't seem as impressed. "Well, sacred or not, I still think we should leave before something bad happens."

Before Charlie could respond, there was a sudden noise from the entrance—a low growl that made all three of them freeze. They turned slowly, expecting to see Bucky standing there, but the bear remained outside, pacing near the tree line.

The growl came again, louder this time. It wasn't Bucky—it was something else, something inside the building.

Charlie's heart raced. "What was that?"

Ella's face paled as she backed away from the carvings. "I don't know, but I don't think we're alone."

The growl echoed through the stone walls again, and this time, it was followed by the unmistakable sound of footsteps—heavy, deliberate footsteps that seemed to be getting closer.

Ben's face drained of color. "We need to get out of here. *Now.*"

Charlie didn't argue. The three of them bolted toward the entrance, their footsteps echoing off the stone floor as they ran. The sound of whatever was inside the building followed them, growing louder with each step. Charlie's mind raced—was it another animal? Something else? He didn't want to find out.

They burst out of the stone structure, stumbling into the snowy clearing. Bucky was still there, watching them intently, but he made no move to approach. Instead, he seemed to be waiting for them to make the next move.

Charlie skidded to a stop beside the bear, panting heavily. "What... what was that?"

Ben, who was now visibly shaking, pointed back toward the building. "We need to leave. I don't care what Bucky wants, we're not sticking around to find out."

Ella, though shaken, stood beside Charlie, her eyes wide with curiosity. "Wait. What if Bucky's protecting us? What if he's been trying to keep us away from that thing inside?"

Charlie's mind raced as he tried to make sense of everything. Bucky had led them here, but he had also kept his distance from the stone structure, as if he knew something dangerous was inside. Maybe Ella was right—maybe Bucky wasn't a threat. Maybe he was a protector.

As they stood there, catching their breath, Bucky let out a soft huff and turned back toward the forest. He glanced over his shoulder, almost as if inviting them to follow him again.

Charlie looked at his friends. "I think we should trust him."

Ben groaned. "Seriously? After all this?"

Ella nodded. "Charlie's right. Bucky's not leading us into danger. He's showing us something, something important."

With no other option, and their hearts still racing, they followed Bucky once more, deeper into the forest, leaving the strange stone structure—and whatever was inside—behind.

Chapter 14: The Great Escape Plan

The snow crunched under their boots as Charlie, Ella, and Ben followed Bucky deeper into the forest, their breaths clouding in the frigid air. The strange stone structure was now far behind them, but the unsettling feeling of being watched had not faded. The growls and footsteps they had heard inside still echoed in Charlie's mind, and he couldn't shake the feeling that whatever was in there had been something they weren't meant to encounter.

Bucky lumbered ahead, his dark shape moving easily through the snow. Though the bear remained silent, there was something purposeful about the way he led them forward, as if he knew exactly where he was taking them.

Charlie glanced at his friends. Ella, who had been full of energy and curiosity, now looked more serious, her brows furrowed as she followed in Bucky's wake. Ben, on the other hand, looked like he was on the verge of panic.

"This has to stop," Ben said, his voice a mix of fear and frustration. "We keep following this bear deeper into the woods, and every time we think we're safe, something else happens. First, he's following us. Then, he leads us to a creepy old ruin. Now what?"

"I know it's scary," Charlie replied, his voice calm but firm. "But Bucky hasn't hurt us. If anything, he's been keeping us safe."

"Safe?" Ben nearly shouted, though he quickly lowered his voice, not wanting to startle the bear. "You call this safe? We're lost in the woods, following a bear! A *bear*, Charlie!"

Ella stepped in, her voice soft but confident. "Ben, I get it. This is scary. But you have to admit, Bucky hasn't done anything to harm us. I think he's trying to protect us."

Ben looked like he wanted to argue, but he sighed instead, his shoulders slumping in defeat. "I just want to get out of here. I don't want to end up as bear food."

Charlie nodded. "I promise we're going to figure this out. We'll find a way back home."

As they followed Bucky further, the forest became denser, the trees taller and more closely packed. The air grew colder, and the sky above darkened with thick, gray clouds. The wind picked up, rustling the branches and sending occasional flurries of snow down on their heads. It was clear that another storm was brewing.

"We need to find shelter before the snow gets worse," Ella said, her eyes scanning the trees.

Just as she spoke, Bucky veered off the path and moved toward a rocky outcrop. At first, it looked like just another pile of snow-covered boulders, but as they got closer, Charlie realized there was something hidden behind it—a narrow opening, almost like the entrance to a cave.

"Do you think Bucky wants us to go in there?" Charlie asked, stepping cautiously toward the opening.

Bucky paused at the entrance to the cave, glancing back at them as if to say, *Yes, follow me.*

Ben shook his head, backing up a step. "No way. I'm not going into some dark cave with a bear."

Ella knelt down beside the entrance, peering inside. "It's not that deep. I think it's just a small shelter. We can wait out the storm in here."

Charlie nodded. "It might be our best option. We can't stay out in the open much longer."

Reluctantly, Ben followed as they all ducked inside the cave. The space was tight, but it was big enough for all of them to sit comfortably. The stone walls were cold to the touch, but at least they were protected from the wind and snow.

Bucky settled himself at the entrance of the cave, blocking most of the cold wind from coming in. The bear let out a deep sigh, as if he, too, was glad to find some respite from the worsening weather.

"We're really doing this," Ben muttered, his arms wrapped tightly around himself for warmth. "Hiding out in a cave with a bear."

"It could be worse," Ella said, her tone light but reassuring. "At least we're out of the storm, and we've got Bucky keeping watch."

Charlie nodded in agreement, though he couldn't help but wonder what Bucky's next move would be. The bear had led them to the cave, but what would happen once the storm passed? Would he continue to lead them deeper into the forest, or would he finally leave them alone?

They sat in silence for a while, huddled together for warmth as the storm outside grew fiercer. The wind howled through the trees, and snow began to pile up at the cave entrance. Despite the tension in the air, the cave offered them a strange sense of security. The world outside seemed distant, and for the first time in hours, Charlie felt like they could rest without fear.

But even as the storm raged outside, Charlie couldn't stop thinking about the stone structure they had left behind. What had been inside? What had Bucky wanted them to find? The bear's behavior was still a mystery, but something deep inside Charlie told him that this wasn't over.

After what felt like hours, the storm began to calm. The howling wind outside softened to a whisper, and the heavy snowfall slowed to a gentle flurry. The gray clouds above began to thin, revealing patches of dark sky.

Ella was the first to stand, stretching her legs and peeking outside. "Looks like the worst of it is over. We should get moving."

Charlie stood as well, glancing at Bucky, who had remained at the entrance of the cave the entire time. The bear seemed calm, almost relaxed, as if he had known the storm would pass soon.

Ben, though still apprehensive, joined them at the cave's entrance. "I hope we're heading back toward civilization this time."

Charlie smiled. "That's the plan."

They stepped out of the cave into a landscape transformed by the snowstorm. The forest was blanketed in fresh powder, and the trees were heavy with snow, their branches bending under the weight. Everything was quiet, almost serene.

Bucky stood up, stretching his massive body as he prepared to lead them once again. But this time, Charlie had a different idea.

"Wait," Charlie said, turning to face the bear. "I think it's time we figure out how to get home. We've followed you this far, but we need to find our way back."

Bucky looked at Charlie, his dark eyes filled with intelligence, as if he understood what Charlie was saying. The bear huffed softly and turned, looking back toward the direction they had come from.

Charlie exchanged a glance with Ella and Ben. "I think Bucky's taking us home."

Ella smiled. "Looks like our adventure is almost over."

Ben, though still wary of the bear, couldn't hide the relief in his voice. "Finally."

With renewed hope, they followed Bucky as he led them back through the forest, retracing their steps through the snow. The bear moved with purpose, as if he knew exactly where he was going, and Charlie felt a sense of peace wash over him. They were going to make it home.

Chapter 15: A Frozen Forest Maze

The forest was eerily quiet as Charlie, Ella, Ben, and Bucky moved through the snow-covered landscape. The storm had left behind a thick blanket of white that made everything look untouched, as if the world had been reset. The trees, bent under the weight of snow, cast long shadows across the forest floor, creating a maze of dark and light that made it hard to tell which way was which.

Bucky led the way, his massive paws sinking into the snow with each step. Charlie, Ella, and Ben followed closely, their breaths coming out in visible puffs of cold air. The silence of the forest was unsettling, broken only by the crunching of their footsteps and the occasional creak of the trees in the wind.

Charlie kept glancing at Bucky, marveling at how the bear seemed to know exactly where he was going. They had been following him for what felt like hours, winding through the forest, up and down small hills, and around clusters of trees that looked like they had been standing for centuries. Charlie wasn't sure if they were truly on the right path, but Bucky's sense of direction gave him hope.

"I think we're getting close to the stream again," Charlie said, trying to sound confident. "If we can cross it safely, we'll be back on track."

Ella nodded, though she was clearly exhausted from the long trek. "I hope you're right. This snow is so deep, it's like walking through quicksand."

Ben, who had been unusually quiet, muttered from the back of the group, "I still can't believe we're trusting a bear to lead us home. This has to be the weirdest Christmas ever."

Charlie couldn't argue with that. Their plan to have a simple Christmas camping trip had turned into something far beyond anything they had imagined. And yet, despite everything, Charlie felt a strange sense of calm. They were still alive, still together, and somehow, Bucky had been looking out for them.

As they continued to walk, the trees began to close in around them, their branches heavy with snow and ice. The forest had become a maze, the path forward winding unpredictably as they tried to navigate the thick undergrowth and avoid getting lost. The snow clung to everything, making it hard to distinguish one direction from another.

"Are we lost?" Ben asked, his voice laced with anxiety.

"No," Charlie replied, though he wasn't entirely sure. "Bucky knows where he's going."

But as they pressed deeper into the forest, even Charlie began to doubt their direction. The landscape had changed so much since the storm that it was hard to tell if they were retracing their steps or heading in an entirely new direction. Everything looked the same—snow, trees, and shadows.

Ella stopped for a moment, catching her breath. "I don't recognize any of this. Are we sure we're not just wandering in circles?"

Before Charlie could respond, Bucky suddenly paused, sniffing the air. The bear's body tensed, his dark eyes scanning the forest around them. It was as if Bucky had sensed something they couldn't see.

Charlie's heart skipped a beat. "What's wrong?"

Bucky let out a low growl and turned sharply, leading them off the path they had been following. He moved quickly now, his movements more urgent than before. Charlie and the others hurried to keep up, struggling through the deep snow.

"What is he doing?" Ben asked, his voice trembling. "Why is he going this way?"

"I don't know," Charlie admitted, his heart racing. "But we have to trust him."

Bucky pushed through the dense forest, weaving between the trees with surprising speed. It was as if he knew something was wrong, and the urgency in his movements made Charlie's pulse quicken. The bear's instincts had been right so far, but this sudden shift in pace had Charlie on edge.

They stumbled after Bucky for what felt like an eternity, the snow slowing their progress and sapping their strength. Every step felt like a battle, but Bucky never stopped or slowed down, his focus fixed on something ahead. It wasn't long before the group realized why.

As they crested a small hill, they found themselves at the edge of the frozen stream once again. The wide expanse of ice stretched out before them, gleaming in the fading light of the afternoon. Charlie's breath caught in his throat—this was their way home.

But the stream looked different now. The ice was darker in places, and cracks spidered across the surface, making it clear that the storm had weakened it. Charlie could feel his heart sink. Crossing it was going to be dangerous.

"We can't go across that," Ben said, his voice trembling with fear. "It's going to break!"

Ella stared at the stream, her face pale but determined. "We don't have a choice. We have to cross it if we want to get home."

Charlie agreed, but the sight of the cracks made him hesitate. If they weren't careful, the ice could give way beneath them, plunging them into the freezing water below. "We'll have to go slow, one at a time. Spread out so we don't put too much pressure on the ice."

Bucky stood at the edge of the stream, watching them intently. The bear didn't move, as if sensing the danger ahead. Charlie glanced at him, wondering if Bucky would even attempt to cross. Bears weren't known for navigating ice, but Bucky had proven to be anything but ordinary.

"I'll go first," Charlie said, stepping forward cautiously.

He tested the ice with his foot, feeling it shift slightly under his weight. The surface creaked ominously, but it held. Taking a deep breath, he stepped onto the frozen stream, moving slowly and keeping his weight distributed as evenly as possible. Every step felt like a gamble, but so far, the ice seemed to be holding.

"Okay," Charlie called back to the others. "It's holding for now, but be careful."

Ella followed, her movements careful and precise. She kept her eyes fixed on the ice beneath her feet, her heart pounding as she made her way across the stream. The ice groaned beneath her, but it held.

Ben, however, was less confident. He stood at the edge, staring down at the cracks in the ice with wide eyes. "I can't do it," he whispered. "It's going to break. I know it."

"You can do this, Ben," Charlie called from the other side, his voice steady. "Just take it slow."

Ben swallowed hard, his hands shaking as he stepped onto the ice. He moved tentatively, each step more hesitant than the last. The ice creaked louder beneath his weight, and the cracks beneath him began to spread.

"Keep going!" Ella urged. "You're almost there!"

But just as Ben was halfway across, the ice gave a loud crack, and a section beneath him splintered. Ben let out a panicked cry as the ice shifted, his feet slipping out from under him.

"Ben!" Charlie shouted, rushing toward the edge of the stream, his heart racing.

But before Charlie could move, Bucky leapt forward. The bear's massive paws struck the ice with surprising grace, and in one swift motion, Bucky pushed Ben back toward the edge of the stream, his powerful body keeping Ben from falling through the broken ice.

Ben scrambled onto solid ground, gasping for breath, his face pale with shock. "I—I thought I was done for."

Bucky let out a soft huff, as if reassuring him, before returning to the far side of the stream, where he waited patiently for the others to cross.

Charlie and Ella hurried to help Ben to his feet, their hearts still racing. "That was too close," Charlie said, shaking his head.

Ben nodded, still catching his breath. "I thought... I thought he was going to leave me."

Ella smiled, relief flooding her face. "Bucky's been looking out for us this whole time. He's not going to leave us behind."

As they all gathered on the far side of the stream, the realization hit them: they were almost home. Bucky had guided them through the most dangerous part of the forest, and now, the path ahead seemed clearer.

63

Chapter 16: The Christmas Eve Rescue

The sun had started its slow descent toward the horizon, casting long shadows across the snow-covered forest. The fading light turned the sky a soft pink and gold, a reminder that night—and Christmas Eve—was fast approaching. Charlie, Ella, and Ben stood on the far side of the frozen stream, their hearts still pounding from the close call. The relief of making it across alive filled the air, but they knew they weren't home yet.

Bucky, who had led them through the forest with such care and focus, now stood silently beside the trees, his dark eyes watching them intently. Charlie looked at the bear with a mixture of gratitude and awe. Bucky had been their protector, their guide, and somehow, despite the fear they'd felt, they had come to trust him completely.

"We're so close now," Charlie said, his breath visible in the cold air. "I think we're almost back to where we started."

Ella looked around, her eyes scanning the familiar layout of the trees. "Yeah, I recognize this place. We camped not far from here when we first arrived. We just need to follow the stream for a bit longer."

Ben, who had regained some of his composure after his terrifying slip on the ice, nodded. "Let's hope we don't run into any more trouble. I've had enough excitement for one Christmas."

With a shared sense of determination, they began to follow the path along the stream, their steps careful but sure. The snow crunched beneath their boots, and the cold air bit at their faces, but there was something comforting about the journey now. They knew they were on the right track, and the prospect of being home—just in time for Christmas—filled them with a renewed energy.

As they walked, Charlie's thoughts kept drifting back to Bucky. The bear had been a mystery from the start, but now it seemed like Bucky had some kind of purpose, as if leading them to safety was part of a plan. He glanced back at the bear, who followed them at a distance, never too far away but keeping a respectful space.

"What do you think will happen to Bucky?" Charlie asked, breaking the silence.

Ella looked thoughtful. "I'm not sure. Maybe he'll go back to wherever he came from once we're safe. He's done his part, hasn't he?"

Ben, though still wary of the bear, nodded in agreement. "Yeah. I mean, as long as he doesn't follow us home, I think we'll be fine."

Charlie smiled faintly, though part of him felt sad at the idea of saying goodbye to Bucky. The bear had been their unexpected ally through the most dangerous part of their journey, and Charlie couldn't shake the feeling that there was more to Bucky's presence than they understood.

They continued along the stream, the sun dipping lower in the sky with each passing minute. The forest was quiet, save for the occasional rustling of wind through the trees and the distant call of a bird. The snow-covered landscape seemed to stretch endlessly, but the growing sense of familiarity reassured them that they were nearing their campsite.

Then, just as the last light of the day began to fade, a sound broke through the quiet—a distant, rhythmic hum that Charlie instantly recognized. It was the sound of an engine.

"Do you hear that?" Ella asked, her eyes widening with hope.

Charlie nodded, his heart racing. "It sounds like a snowmobile!"

Ben, who had been trailing behind, rushed to catch up. "Do you think it's a rescue team? They might be looking for us!"

Without another word, they quickened their pace, their exhaustion forgotten in the surge of excitement. The sound of the engine grew louder, and soon, they could see a faint light cutting through the trees ahead.

As they rounded the bend in the stream, the forest opened up into a familiar clearing—the place where they had first set up camp. And there, waiting for them, were two snowmobiles, their headlights cutting through the growing darkness. A small group of people stood beside them, bundled up in thick winter coats, scanning the forest as if searching for something.

Charlie's heart leaped with joy as he recognized one of the figures. "It's them! It's my dad!"

He broke into a run, shouting as he waved his arms. "Dad! Over here!"

The group by the snowmobiles turned at the sound of Charlie's voice, and in an instant, they were rushing forward to meet them. Charlie's father, his face lined with worry and relief, enveloped his son in a tight hug as soon as he reached him.

"We've been looking for you for hours," his father said, his voice thick with emotion. "We thought you were lost for good!"

"We're okay," Charlie replied, his voice muffled against his father's coat. "We made it."

Ella's parents rushed to her, wrapping her in a warm embrace, while Ben's older brother, who had been part of the rescue team, clapped him on the shoulder.

"You guys had us all worried," Ben's brother said, shaking his head. "What happened out there?"

Before they could answer, Charlie glanced back toward the trees. "We... we had help," he said, his eyes searching the shadows for Bucky. But the bear, who had been following them so closely for so long, was nowhere to be seen.

"He was right behind us," Ella said, turning to look around. "Where did he go?"

Charlie's father frowned, confused. "Who are you talking about?"

Charlie hesitated, unsure how to explain. "Bucky. The bear. He's been following us—leading us—this whole time."

"A bear?" Ben's brother asked, his brow furrowed. "You mean you've been out here with a bear following you?"

Ben nodded, though he still looked uneasy. "Yeah. But he wasn't dangerous. He helped us get back."

Charlie's father shook his head in disbelief. "I don't know what to say. A bear guiding you? That sounds... incredible."

"It was," Ella said softly. "He saved us more than once."

But as they looked into the woods, there was no sign of Bucky. The bear had disappeared, leaving them alone now that they were safe.

"Maybe he knew his job was done," Charlie said quietly, a hint of sadness in his voice.

The adults exchanged puzzled glances, but they didn't press the issue. The relief of finding the kids safe and sound outweighed any questions they had about a mysterious bear guiding them through the wilderness.

As they loaded onto the snowmobiles and prepared to head home, Charlie couldn't help but glance back one last time at the edge of the forest. Somewhere, deep in the shadows, he hoped Bucky was watching, keeping an eye on them.

The snowmobiles roared to life, and as they sped across the snowy landscape, Charlie felt a deep sense of gratitude for their unexpected Christmas adventure. It hadn't been the holiday they had planned, but it had become something far more magical than they could have ever imagined.

They were going home for Christmas, and they owed it all to Bucky.

Chapter 17: Saying Goodbye to Bucky

The snowmobiles raced through the snowy forest, the trees flying past in a blur as the wind whipped at their faces. Charlie, Ella, and Ben huddled close for warmth as they held tight to the handles of the sleds. The relief of being rescued was still fresh in their minds, but something else weighed on their hearts—Bucky was gone.

Charlie couldn't stop thinking about the bear, the way he had watched over them, led them to safety, and then disappeared without a trace. As they rode through the snow, he kept glancing back toward the forest, hoping for one last glimpse of Bucky, though he knew the bear was unlikely to show himself again.

They had spent so much time fearing Bucky at first, unsure of his intentions, but now it felt strange to leave him behind. Charlie had grown to trust the bear in ways he never thought possible, and the thought of never seeing him again made his heart ache.

As the snowmobiles slowed down, Ella leaned close to Charlie and said, "Do you think we'll ever see him again?"

Charlie didn't know how to answer. He wanted to believe that somehow, Bucky would find his way back into their lives, but deep down, he knew the forest was where Bucky belonged. "I don't know," Charlie said, his voice soft. "But I hope so."

Ben, who had been riding quietly behind them, chimed in. "I don't think I'll ever forget him. I mean, how many people can say they were guided through the woods by a bear?"

Ella smiled faintly. "Yeah, it's not exactly a normal Christmas story, is it?"

Charlie's father, who was driving the snowmobile, overheard their conversation and chuckled. "A bear leading you to safety on Christmas Eve? It's the kind of story people would never believe if they didn't know you kids."

Charlie smiled, but his thoughts remained on Bucky. The ride continued in silence as the snowmobiles moved closer to the edge of the forest, the world around them growing more familiar. They were heading back toward the town, back toward warmth, safety, and their families. But the magic of the forest, and of Bucky's unexpected friendship, lingered in the air.

After what felt like hours, they finally arrived at the edge of the woods. The snowmobiles slowed to a stop, and in the distance, Charlie could see the soft glow of the town's Christmas lights twinkling through the falling snow. They had made it. They were home.

Charlie, Ella, and Ben climbed off the sleds, stretching their legs and taking in the sight of their familiar surroundings. The snow-covered rooftops and the festive decorations made the town look like something out of a Christmas postcard, but after everything they had been through, it felt surreal.

"We're home," Ella whispered, a sense of wonder in her voice.

Ben nodded, his face full of relief. "I can't believe we made it."

Charlie's father turned to them, a smile of pure relief on his face. "You kids gave us quite a scare, but I'm just glad you're safe."

Charlie smiled back, grateful to be home, but there was still something missing. He glanced back toward the dark forest behind them, his heart heavy with the knowledge that Bucky was still out there, watching over them from the shadows.

As if reading his thoughts, Ella placed a hand on Charlie's shoulder. "Do you think he knows we're okay now?"

Charlie nodded slowly. "Yeah, I think he knows. He was watching over us the whole time."

Ben, who had been quiet for a moment, looked back at the trees as well. "Do you think he's... like, magic or something?"

Charlie shrugged, unsure of how to explain it. "I don't know. But there's definitely something special about him."

Ella smiled, a twinkle in her eyes. "Maybe he's the forest's guardian, looking out for anyone who gets lost."

"I'd like to think that," Charlie said softly. "Maybe he was meant to help us."

Just as they were about to turn and head toward town, a soft sound echoed through the trees—the unmistakable huff of a bear. Charlie's heart skipped a beat, and he turned sharply toward the forest, his eyes scanning the shadows. And there, standing at the edge of the trees, half-hidden in the shadows, was Bucky.

The bear's dark eyes gleamed in the fading light, and for a moment, Charlie felt as though Bucky was saying goodbye. The bear stood still, watching them with the same calm, protective gaze he had carried throughout their journey.

Charlie smiled, his heart swelling with gratitude. "There he is," he whispered to Ella and Ben, who both turned to see Bucky standing in the shadows.

Ben's eyes widened. "He came to say goodbye."

Ella's face softened. "He's watching over us, even now."

Charlie took a deep breath and waved at the bear, his heart full. "Thank you, Bucky," he said softly, his voice barely a whisper. "Thank you for everything."

Bucky huffed again, as if in response, before turning and disappearing into the forest. The trees swallowed him up, and just like that, he was gone. But the sense of peace he left behind stayed with them, filling the air with a quiet kind of magic.

Charlie, Ella, and Ben stood in silence for a moment longer, their eyes lingering on the spot where Bucky had disappeared. It felt like the end of an era, the end of an adventure they would never forget.

"Do you think he'll be okay?" Ella asked, her voice soft.

Charlie smiled, a sense of certainty filling him. "Yeah. He's where he belongs now."

As they turned to head toward town, the glow of the Christmas lights grew brighter, and the familiar sounds of laughter and holiday music reached their ears. They were home, and the warmth of their families and the magic of Christmas waited for them just ahead.

But even as they stepped back into the world of warmth and light, Charlie knew that the forest—and Bucky—would always be a part of them. The adventure they had shared with the bear had changed them, and the memories of their time in the woods would stay with them forever.

Chapter 18: Home for Christmas

The walk back into town felt like stepping into a dream. The soft glow of the Christmas lights reflected off the snow, turning the world into a sparkling winter wonderland. The sound of laughter and holiday music filled the air as people hurried through the streets, bundled in scarves and hats, carrying bags full of presents. It was Christmas Eve, and despite everything Charlie, Ella, and Ben had been through, they were finally home.

Charlie's father led them down the main street toward his house, which was warmly lit, its windows glowing with the soft flicker of candles. The familiar sights of town—shops decorated with wreaths, the towering Christmas tree in the town square—felt strange after their adventure in the woods. It was as if they had stepped out of one world and into another.

As they approached Charlie's house, his mother rushed out to meet them, her face flushed with worry and relief. "Oh, thank goodness!" she exclaimed, throwing her arms around Charlie. "I've been so worried! Are you alright?"

Charlie hugged his mother tightly, feeling the warmth of her embrace seep into his cold bones. "We're fine, Mom. We had a bit of an adventure, but we made it back."

Ella's and Ben's parents were already there, embracing their children and thanking the rescue team for bringing them home. There were tears of relief, joyful hugs, and grateful words exchanged, but beneath it all, there was a sense of quiet awe about what the three friends had experienced in the woods.

After what felt like a whirlwind of hugs and questions, Charlie, Ella, and Ben finally settled inside Charlie's house, sitting in the cozy living room with mugs of hot chocolate in their hands. The Christmas tree sparkled with lights and ornaments, and stockings were hung by the fireplace, creating the perfect holiday scene. It felt surreal after the days they had spent navigating the wild, freezing forest.

"This feels so strange," Ella said, sipping her hot chocolate as she stared at the tree. "I mean, it's Christmas Eve, and we're finally home, but it feels like we were in a completely different world out there."

Ben, who was sitting next to the fireplace, nodded. "Yeah. One minute we're fighting off the cold and following a bear through the forest, and now... we're sitting here, like nothing ever happened."

Charlie smiled, though his thoughts kept drifting back to Bucky and the forest. "It's like we stepped out of a story. But it's real. We'll never forget what happened out there."

His mother, who had been bustling around the kitchen, came in with a tray of cookies and set it on the coffee table. "I'm just so thankful you're all safe," she said with a warm smile. "It sounds like you had quite the adventure."

Charlie glanced at his parents, wondering how much they'd believe about what had really happened. How could he explain the bond they had formed with Bucky? Or the strange stone structure deep in the forest? It felt like a story too wild to tell.

"Yeah, it was definitely an adventure," Charlie said, choosing his words carefully.

His father sat down beside him, his eyes filled with curiosity. "Your mom and I were talking, and we'd like to hear the full story—when you're ready."

Charlie glanced at Ella and Ben, who exchanged knowing looks. They had agreed on the way back that Bucky's role in their adventure might sound too fantastical to share, at least with adults who hadn't seen it firsthand. But maybe they didn't need to explain everything just yet.

"We'll tell you all about it tomorrow," Charlie said with a smile. "But for now, can we just enjoy Christmas Eve?"

His parents smiled and nodded, understanding that the kids needed some time to process everything that had happened. "Of course," his mother said, pulling him into another hug. "You're home now, and that's all that matters."

As the night wore on, the house filled with the familiar warmth and laughter of Christmas Eve. They exchanged small gifts, snacked on Christmas cookies, and listened to carols playing softly in the background. It was the kind of peaceful, magical night that felt like a dream after everything they had been through.

But even as they celebrated, there was a part of Charlie that couldn't stop thinking about Bucky. The bear had been more than just an animal. He had been a guide, a protector, and somehow, a friend. Charlie wondered if Bucky was still out there, watching the town from the shadows of the forest, ensuring they were safe.

Later that evening, as the fire in the fireplace began to die down and the house grew quiet, Charlie slipped away from the living room and out onto the front porch. The night was cold, and the stars twinkled brightly in the sky. The snow-covered landscape sparkled under the moonlight, and the soft hum of Christmas lights filled the air with a peaceful glow.

Charlie wrapped his coat tightly around him and stared out toward the edge of the forest. Somewhere out there, in the quiet woods, Bucky was waiting—watching, maybe even resting after his long journey with them. The thought brought a smile to Charlie's face.

As he stood there, lost in thought, Ella and Ben joined him on the porch, both of them bundled up against the cold.

"Thinking about Bucky?" Ella asked with a soft smile.

Charlie nodded, his eyes still fixed on the distant trees. "Yeah. I wonder if we'll ever see him again."

Ben leaned against the porch railing, his breath visible in the cold air. "You think he'll come back?"

"I don't know," Charlie replied, his voice quiet. "But I like to think he'll always be out there, looking out for the forest—and maybe for us too."

Ella nodded in agreement. "He was more than just a bear, wasn't he? It felt like he was guiding us, like he knew exactly what we needed."

Ben smiled, though there was still a hint of disbelief in his voice. "I can't believe we actually followed a bear through the woods and survived. I mean, who does that?"

Charlie chuckled. "Yeah, it's a Christmas we'll never forget."

As the three friends stood together, staring out at the snow-covered forest, a sense of peace washed over them. They had faced the unknown, trusted each other, and discovered something magical in the heart of the wilderness. It hadn't been the Christmas they had planned, but it had become something far more special.

Chapter 19: The Gift of Adventure

Christmas morning dawned bright and clear, with the sun shining over the snow-covered town, making everything sparkle. Inside Charlie's house, the scent of freshly baked cinnamon rolls filled the air, and the sound of carols drifted softly from the radio. It was the kind of peaceful Christmas morning that felt like it belonged in a storybook.

But for Charlie, Ella, and Ben, the events of the past few days were still fresh in their minds. As they gathered in the living room to exchange gifts with their families, there was a quiet bond between the three friends—something unspoken, a shared understanding of the adventure they had experienced together. It was as if the magic of the forest and Bucky's presence had left an indelible mark on them.

Charlie sat on the floor by the Christmas tree, unwrapping a present from his parents—a brand-new set of hiking boots. He smiled, knowing that they were meant for future adventures, though he couldn't help but think of the boots he'd worn through the snow during their journey.

"These will come in handy," he said, holding them up for his parents to see.

His father chuckled. "We thought you could use a new pair after all that hiking."

Ella, who was sitting beside him, grinned. "Looks like they're preparing you for the next adventure."

Charlie smiled, but his thoughts were already drifting back to the forest. There was something about being out there, in the heart of nature, that had felt more real than anything else. The magic of the trees, the quiet of the snow, and the mysterious bond they had formed with Bucky—all of it had changed him in ways he hadn't fully understood yet.

Ben, who was sitting across from them, unwrapped a small, solar-powered camping lantern from his brother. He held it up with a grin. "Well, at least I'll be prepared next time we end up in the middle of nowhere."

Ella laughed, her face glowing with happiness as she unwrapped a sketchbook and colored pencils from her parents. "I'm definitely sketching the forest as soon as I can. I've got so many memories I want to put on paper."

The three friends exchanged smiles, knowing that no matter how many gifts they received or how much laughter filled the room, the greatest gift they had received this Christmas was the adventure they had shared. It wasn't about the presents under the tree or the festive decorations—it was about the bond they had formed, the challenges they had faced together, and the magical moments they had experienced in the wild.

After breakfast, Charlie, Ella, and Ben stepped outside to enjoy the crisp winter air. The snow glistened under the bright sunlight, and the town was peaceful, with only the faint sound of distant carolers filling the air. They walked down the quiet street, their boots crunching in the snow, as they headed toward the edge of the forest.

"We never really told anyone the full story," Ella said, glancing at the trees in the distance. "About Bucky, I mean."

Charlie shook his head. "I don't think they'd believe us. A bear guiding us through the woods? It sounds like something out of a fairy tale."

Ben kicked at the snow, his face thoughtful. "Maybe it's better that way. Some things are just meant to stay between us."

Charlie smiled. "Yeah, I think you're right. It's our adventure. And no one can take that away from us."

They reached the edge of the forest, the place where Bucky had last appeared before disappearing into the trees. The familiar path stretched out before them, winding through the snow-covered landscape, and for a moment, they stood in silence, each of them lost in their thoughts.

Ella pulled out her sketchbook and began to draw, her pencil gliding across the page as she captured the beauty of the forest. Ben, who had been quietly watching, turned to Charlie. "Do you think we'll ever see him again?"

Charlie glanced at the trees, the memory of Bucky still fresh in his mind. "I don't know. But even if we don't, I know he'll always be out there, watching over the forest."

Ella smiled as she added the finishing touches to her sketch. "Maybe that's the magic of it. Bucky was never really ours to keep. He belongs to the woods."

Charlie nodded, feeling a deep sense of peace. "Yeah. He's part of the forest. And so are we now, in a way."

The three friends stood there for a while longer, watching the forest, remembering the adventure that had brought them closer than ever before. The snow sparkled in the sunlight, and the trees swayed gently in the breeze, as if whispering secrets only they could hear.

After a while, Ella closed her sketchbook and tucked it under her arm. "We should head back. Our families are probably waiting for us."

Charlie and Ben nodded, but before they turned to leave, Charlie looked back at the forest one last time. He didn't see Bucky, but he felt the bear's presence, a quiet strength that seemed to watch over them from afar. It was comforting, knowing that Bucky was still out there, somewhere in the wild.

As they walked back toward town, Charlie felt a sense of gratitude for everything they had experienced. The adventure, the challenges, the moments of fear and wonder—it had all been part of something bigger, something magical. And though the forest was behind them, the memories would stay with them forever.

Later that afternoon, as they sat around the fireplace, their families laughing and sharing stories, Charlie, Ella, and Ben exchanged knowing glances. They didn't need to explain what they had been through. The adventure was theirs, a gift they would carry with them always.

Chapter 20: The Spirit of the Woods

Christmas Day melted into the late afternoon, and the glow of the setting sun painted the sky in brilliant hues of pink and orange. Charlie, Ella, and Ben sat together on the porch, the day's excitement beginning to wind down. Inside, the warmth of family celebrations continued, but the three friends found solace in the quiet outdoors, watching the snow sparkle in the fading light.

"I still can't believe we made it back," Ben said, staring out at the forest. His tone was soft, reflective. "It feels like the woods were a different world."

Ella, ever thoughtful, nodded as she looked at the edge of the trees. "We went on an adventure we never expected. And honestly, I think it changed us."

Charlie didn't say anything for a moment. He felt it too—the subtle shift in all of them since returning from the forest. There was something unspoken but undeniable between the three of them. They had shared a unique bond with the wilderness, and with Bucky, that no one else could fully understand.

He leaned back in his chair and exhaled slowly. "It's like we've seen something... more. Something bigger than just us."

Ella smiled at his words. "You know, I don't think we'll ever see the forest the same way again."

Ben chuckled softly. "Especially with a giant bear roaming around in there."

Charlie's lips twitched into a smile. "Yeah. But I don't think Bucky was just any bear. He was more like... a guardian."

Ben leaned back, his voice softer now. "Do you think anyone would believe us if we told them? About Bucky, I mean?"

Ella shook her head, her expression full of wonder. "Probably not. But that's okay. This adventure was for us."

Charlie agreed. They had learned something about trust, survival, and the wild beauty of the world around them. Bucky had guided them when they were lost, protected them when they were vulnerable, and showed them that the forest held secrets far beyond anything they could have imagined. He had been a guardian, not just of the forest, but of them too.

For a while, they sat in comfortable silence, the soft crunch of snow under passing footsteps and the distant hum of Christmas music from nearby houses filling the air. The world felt peaceful, and for the first time in days, they felt truly at ease.

As the last rays of sunlight dipped behind the horizon, Ella turned to Charlie and Ben. "What do you think will happen next? With Bucky, I mean."

Charlie's eyes wandered back to the trees. The forest, so familiar yet now steeped in mystery, seemed alive with untold stories. "I don't know. But I like to think he's still out there, watching over the woods. And maybe... maybe he'll help others who get lost, just like he helped us."

Ben nodded thoughtfully. "Yeah. He's like the spirit of the woods or something. Always there, always watching."

Charlie smiled, his heart full of gratitude. "We were lucky to meet him."

As they continued to sit together, watching the sky darken and the stars begin to twinkle overhead, something strange and magical happened. A soft, distant sound echoed through the night—a low, rumbling huff, carried on the cold winter breeze. The sound was unmistakable.

"Did you hear that?" Ella whispered, her eyes wide with wonder.

Charlie nodded, his heart skipping a beat. "It's Bucky."

Ben grinned, shaking his head in disbelief. "I thought we'd never hear from him again."

But there it was—Bucky's unmistakable huff, like a gentle reminder that he was still out there, watching from the shadows, a silent guardian of the forest. It was as if he was saying goodbye one last time, acknowledging the bond they had shared.

The three friends exchanged a look, and in that moment, they knew—this adventure would stay with them forever. The lessons they had learned, the courage they had found, and the friendship they had formed with the wild and mysterious bear had changed them in ways they couldn't yet fully understand.